WIT

THE COMFORT OF HIS ARMS

"W-what are you doing? Put me down." Her protest sounded weak even to her own ears. She could not deny that she felt safe in the man's arms.

"You should not have come, my lady. 'Tis too soon since your accident."

Rose wanted to protest again, yet the strange dizziness persisted. Despite her better judgment, she relaxed against him. "I think it was only the bumpy halt that startled me, Sterling. If you give me a few moments, I shall be able to manage to ride back unassisted."

"We are going back to the Hall at once, my lady."

Rose didn't argue as he took Vesta's reins from her hand. He turned the stallion round and walked the animals back to the rear gate. Every nerve in her body seemed to be aware of his masculine appeal. The scent of his sandalwood soap, the feeling of those strong muscular arms guiding his horse, the coarse texture of his coat against her cheek, and the sinewy strength of his legs where hers dangled. She'd never been held so close by a man and her senses were reeling. . . .

WITHDRAWN

Books by Lynn Collum

A GAME OF CHANCE

ELIZABETH AND THE MAJOR

THE SPY'S BRIDE

LADY MIRANDA'S MASQUERADE

THE CHRISTMAS CHARM

THE VALENTINE CHARM

THE WEDDING CHARM

MISS WHITING AND THE SEVEN WARDS

A KISS AT MIDNIGHT

Published by Zebra Books

A KISS AT MIDNIGHT

Lynn Collum

ZEBRA BOOKS
Kensington Publishing Corp.
http://www.kensingtonbooks.com

ZEBRA BOOKS are published by

Kensington Publishing Corp.
850 Third Avenue
New York, NY 10022

Copyright © 2002 by Jerry Lynn Smith

All rights reserved. No part of this book may be reproduced in any form or by any means without the prior written consent of the Publisher, excepting brief quotes used in reviews.

If you purchased this book without a cover you should be aware that this book is stolen property. It was reported as "unsold and destroyed" to the Publisher and neither the Author nor the Publisher has received any payment for this "stripped book."

All Kensington titles, imprints and distributed lines are available at special quantity discounts for bulk purchases for sales promotion, premiums, fund-raising, educational or institutional use.

Special book excerpts or customized printings can also be created to fit specific needs. For details, write or phone the office of the Kensington Special Sales Manager: Kensington Publishing Corp., 850 Third Avenue, New York, NY 10022. Attn. Special Sales Department. Phone: 1-800-221-2647.

Zebra and the Z logo Reg. U.S. Pat. & TM Off.

First Printing: November 2002
10 9 8 7 6 5 4 3 2 1

Printed in the United States of America

Prologue

Headstrong daughters were the plague of fathers with mortgaged estates. The Marquess of Denham recognized the signs of such waywardness in his youngest child even before she reached her sixteenth birthday. The problem became evident to his lordship soon after the demise of his wife. Never one to pay heed to his offspring since children were the province of females, the matter came to his attention when the chit repeatedly ignored his rules. A scandal ensued when she raced one of his stallions against Reggie Hollister's well-ribbed gray; the Reverend Mr. Martin caught her in breeches at the horse auction in York; and daily she exceeded the estate boundaries without the company of her groom. Even the Duchess of Rayburn, his nearest neighbor, chastised his lordship at every encounter for his shortcomings as a parent.

In truth, these infractions didn't disturb the marquess, so little did he concern himself with the chit. But the ladies of the neighborhood used the girl's conduct as an excuse to intrude in Lord Denham's affairs. They rarely missed an opportunity to either flirt with him or to urge him to marry again before the girl ruined herself. He soon came to realize there was nothing more horrid than a forty-year-old coquette with marriage on her mind.

Still, it was generally believed that a proper wife could take the girl in hand and end her daring behavior. It wasn't until the duchess told him point blank that he was likely to be stuck with the girl for life if she weren't guarded more closely, that the marquess realized something must be done about the wayward chit. The mere prospect of being forever pestered about Lady Rosamund and her antics spurred him to take action.

But him, remarry? Never! Denham wasn't in the petticoat line. He'd wed for wealth the first time and the union had been rather tumultuous, his wife being a thorn in his side who often criticized how and where he spent money. He was determined not to bring another female into his household, even one with enough blunt to end his current financial woes. Yet the matter of money always pressed on a man with a fondness for the Fancy and little head for the business side of breeding.

The solution to his problem was offered to him one day after he'd had a run of particularly bad luck at the races. As he lamented his woes, Lord Hollister remarked, "Take heart, Denham. You'll be swimming in funds once you find a wealthy husband for that lovely daughter of yours. With her looks the nabobs will be forming a line."

The following morning the marquess truly took a long look at his troublesome young daughter. She possessed a budding female form with golden curls, good teeth, and wide green eyes. As he saw it, her only flaw was her unreserved nature. He took note of how the young men of York gaped at the girl when they attended church. It quickly dawned on him that Lady Rosamund's comeliness could be his salvation, a much more amenable solution to his fiscal woes, since she would be the one to make the sacrifice for the benefit of the estate rather than he. Still in official mourning for the marchioness and being scarcely sixteen, there could be no question of marriage at present. But when the time came he would marry her off to a wealthy man. Until then, he would do what he must to ensure the girl was brought to heel. But the gentleman had neither the time nor the inclination for such a task. That meant subjecting her to the harsh discipline of a proper school.

His lordship sent his solicitor to search England high and low for the school whose rules were strict enough to curb the young lady's wild ways. Parson's Academy for Young Ladies of Quality in Somerset under the harsh directions of Miss Bettina Parson, suited the marquess perfectly. By the end of the week, he sent his protesting daughter with exact instructions to the headmistress on what the lady must accomplish.

Lady Rosamund, furious at her father to be sent from her home, devised a plan on her journey to school. Her brother had been sent down from Oxford for misconduct, so why could she not do the same?

Unfortunately for the young lady, Miss Parson's will made iron look weak. No female had ever been sent home from her academy, especially when there was money to be made. The headmistress informed Lady Rosamund of that fact on her arrival, then sent her to her room.

The clash of wills began at once, but it wasn't just Lady Rosamund against Miss Parson. The girl was against a school of penniless females who valued their positions and they had been given exact instructions. The stern teachers at the school cajoled and punished the marquess' daughter at every turn. She strained against the rigid rules at first, but with no response from her father to a deluge of letters promising to behave and very much disliking the long days working in the kitchens for her misconduct or sitting alone in an attic room, she finally gave in to her fate.

A month passed before she fully accepted the new routine of school life. Walks in the garden and chats with newlymade friends did much to soothe her restless spirit. After several months, she acknowledged that there would be no reprieve from her indifferent parent. Life would be what she made of it. Soon she became a model of propriety with the calming influence of her friends, Miss Sarah Whiting and Miss Ella Sanderson.

Of like age and with equally uninterested relatives the three girls spent many of the school holidays together with only the sour Miss Parson for company. A lasting bond quickly formed, and the three young ladies became inseparable, calling themselves the Three Fates, spinning away the best of their lives in the remote school, or so they thought in their youthful innocence.

As time passed, Lady Rose did little to distress her teachers. The headmistress duly reported her progress to the marquess, mistaking the young lady's docile conduct for rehabilitated ways and not that of someone biding her time until once again free.

Lady Rose's eighteenth birthday came and went without a word from Denham Hall. She began to think that she would reach her majority before her father remembered he possessed a daughter. But the spring that the young lady turned nineteen, Miss Parson surprised all the students of the academy with the announcement that Parson's Academy would close permanently at the end of May, due to her retirement.

For Lady Rose, Sarah, and Ella, the closing was bittersweet. The three had formed a bond closer than many families. Yet each knew the time had come for them to return to their homes and begin their lives. The girls had only to wait and see what fate would spin for them.

As the end of May approached, Lady Rose wondered about her future life at Denham Hall. She was no longer a madcap miss of sixteen who gave not a thought to dashing across the moors at all hours of the day or night. Her life would be very different from the one she'd known, yet she couldn't help but be excited to be going back to Yorkshire.

One

Spring was the busiest time of year at Hillcrest, the ancestral home of Viscount Buckleigh, albeit the gentleman was rarely in residence. Active in politics, he left much of the daily running of his large estate to his eldest son, who, unlike most members of his family, owned a distaste for the idle life of London. In truth, Lord Buckleigh, while praiseworthy in many ways, had little liking for farming and had often left decisions to his steward, an honest man with little imagination or initiative, leaving Hillcrest in need of more progressive leadership, which his lordship's heir willingly provided.

Garth Sterling Fenton, the elder of the viscount's two sons, was in many ways like other fashionable gentlemen of the Ton. A handsome athletic man, he rode well, was a crack shot, drove to an inch, and, in truth, was a complete out-and-outer. But unlike many of his contemporaries, his depth of mind did not allow for days spent worrying about fashion, games of chance, or females of questionable virtue and great beauty. On his entry into Society he soon developed an abiding dislike of being pursued for his family's wealth and title which kept him from the social affairs of Town. To the dismay of matchmaking mothers and eligible young females, the future vis-

count ignored the coquettish glances thrown his way.
Yet what was there for a wealthy young man of twenty
to do with his days? With no great enthusiasm, he'd
sampled the life of the fashionable Buck—shooting
at Manton's Gallery, sparring at Gentleman Jackson's
Academy, gathering at White's and Boodles, racing
his friends to Brighton and even occasionally wagering at one of the fashionable gaming hells. Still he
found himself discontent.

Then an incident occurred which caused only the
briefest stir in Society but affected Garth deeply,
being a minor player in the event. It took place on a
pleasant day spent with friends enjoying a prizefight
just outside of London. The boisterous young gentlemen had returned to Town and repaired to a
tavern where they continued their revels. A dispute
had occurred over the favors of a particularly entic-
ing serving wench who was all too willing to go with
the highest bidder. A rash young earl, deep in his
cups, had pulled his cane sword, slashing the face of
Sir Parks Windom, a young cawker newly arrived in
London to acquire some Town bronze. The disfig-
uring wound needed the services of a surgeon, but
most of the drunken company abandoned the young
man to continue their revels elsewhere, leaving only
Garth to see to the wounded victim. Despite hardly
knowing the young lad from Leeds, Garth felt responsible for not keeping Sir Parks, a lad of no more
than seventeen, from harm, having been the one to
invite him to join their party.

After seeing the young man's wound tended to
and escorting him back to his rooms, Garth made his
way through the damp morning fog pondering the
night's events. The utter triviality of their lifestyle
struck him as his carriage tooled back to Berkeley

Square. Shocked at the callous treatment given to the injured young man by his party of friends, Garth was convinced that there had to be more to life than idling away one's evening in useless pursuit of pleasure that too easily could end in disaster. Sir Parks had survived, but it might have ended in a far darker manner had the foolish man with the hidden sword had his way. In those early morning hours, Garth made a vow to find a way of life that was productive and fulfilling.

To his family's amazement, Garth arrived home informing them of his intent to do what he could to help his father maintain the estate. Lord Buckleigh, delighted to be relieved of the onerous burden, turned over the books to his heir, determined to put all his energies into his first love, politics. The future viscount settled in to his new duties at Hillcrest, never tempted to return to London's yearly fashionable Season.

In the six years of Garth's management, the estate's size doubled as well as the production of wheat, wool, and turnips. Every aspect of Hillcrest ran smoothly from the tenant farms to the home dairy. The only rub in this picture of plenty, in Lady Buckleigh's opinion, remained her son's failure to find a suitable bride. But, then how could he, covered in manure and dirt most days?

To silence his mother's lament which had grown more strident with each passing year, Garth made a promise that if he were not wed by his thirtieth birthday, he would brave the ballrooms of London Society in search of a bride. Yet the prospect did not appeal, since he knew how it would be—flocks of young females all vying to be the future Lady Buckleigh, not caring a fig about him as a man. But at eight-and-twenty, he did not dwell on the matter overmuch, since the event lurked some two years in the future.

Life ran smoothly for the Fenton family at Hillcrest, where Garth resided most of the year, and in London, where Lord and Lady Fenton and Jack spent most of their time. But as with all things, change was inevitable.

On a bright morning in May in the late spring of 1814, one of his lordship's footmen arrived from London with an urgent missive for Garth. He broke the seal and read the lines but the letter gave no details of the problem that so demanded his attention. His black brows drew together, giving his handsome but angular face a stern appearance which might frighten all but those who knew his kind nature. He turned to the servant, who looked very smart in his gray and silver livery. "What is this about, Toby? My father knows I cannot leave the estate with all that must be done before June. Is this some ploy of my mother's to bring me to Town?"

The footman stood as straight as a rod, but his tone was less formal, having known the gentleman since he was in short coats. "There's somethin' not right, sir. I have my suspicions, but the viscount is in high dudgeon and it gots to do with Master Jack."

There was likely no one in England who disliked London more than Garth, but if his younger brother were in trouble, he would go at once. Yet as that thought entered his mind, he couldn't imagine what could have gone wrong that would require his presence. Both his father and mother were in Town for the Season. Something had to be seriously awry for them to interrupt his work.

"Tell Simon to have my curricle readied at once." Garth tossed the letter on his desk and strode from the room.

Within the hour, he was on the road to Town. The journey from Wiltshire took the remainder of the day and it was well after dark when he drew his curricle to a halt in front of the Berkeley Square town house. To his surprise the house looked empty, nearly every window dark. Had his parents and brother gone out for the evening in the middle of this crisis? He would throttle Jack if he had set some disaster in motion, then gone merrily along his way leaving others to clean up the mess.

A single knock and the door was opened by Hickam, the butler, as if he'd been hovering in anticipation of an arrival. With the Fenton family for nearly thirty years, the only testament to the man's aging was that his black hair had grown white, otherwise he was still the slender reserved man who started as footman and worked his way to the supreme position of trust of any household.

"It's good you've come so quickly, sir. I'm that worried about his lordship."

"Is my father ill?" Garth asked as the butler removed his modest three-tiered driving cape.

"Not physically, sir, but heartsick." Hickam draped the gray cape over his arm and led the young master down the hall to the library. After a sharp knock he opened the door for the gentleman and announced, "Mr. Garth is here, my lord."

In contrast to the front hall, the library was well-lit with braces of candles strategically positioned round the room. The viscount and his wife were seated near the tall windows that opened onto a small garden. His lordship's hair had silvered with only a few remaining streaks of brown peppering the curls, but Lady Buckleigh appeared to have found some device to hold nature at bay, for her curls remained as dark as Garth's own. Jack Fenton stood in front of the cold fireplace, a haggard look on his handsome young face, his raven black curls tousled as if he'd run his fingers through them numerous times. Seeing such defeat those in gray eyes, Garth knew a moment's alarm.

"You are here at last." The viscount rose, coming to embrace his son. "It's the Chalice of Naples. It's been stolen."

Garth's gaze flashed to the glass cabinet which housed the treasured cup, but the velvet pedestal stood empty. While the cup was worth a small fortune due to the jewels embedded in the ornate silver stem, for Viscount Buckleigh and all Fentons it was considered a talisman of good luck. Given to the first viscount during the Crusades for saving the heir to the throne during a battle, the King of Naples prophesied that the family's fortunes would flourish as long as the chalice was kept safe. Every proceeding Fenton generation had developed a healthy respect and fondness for the beautiful vessel.

Although not a superstitious person by nature, a strange feeling settled in Garth's stomach as he gazed at the empty cabinet. The chalice was as much a part of the family legacy as Hillcrest. To lose such a familial treasure would be unthinkable. "When was it stolen? Have you informed Bow Street? What has this to do with Jack?"

His brother stepped forward. "I didn't know I couldn't trust the gentleman, Garth."

"What gentleman?" He looked from his brother to his father.

The viscount drew his eldest son over to the cluster of chairs. "Hickam, bring some refreshments for my son."

As Garth reluctantly settled, the viscount gave a heavy sigh. "Let us begin at the beginning. Tuesday night, your mother and I were going to a dinner party at Melbourne House. Jack and a group of his friends were to go to the Theatre Royal for some trumpery play or such, so he asked if he might have them here to dine before they departed. Of course we agreed."

"What friends?" Garth put the question to his brother. He was not unaware that, like many of the younger generation, his brother was not so particular whom he rubbed elbows with as long as they possessed the appearance of wealth and good manners.

Jack ticked off the names. "Albert, Lord Hartson, my oldest friend. Binky Greenwood, Langley's heir and a jolly good fellow, and Sir Henry Kirkland, an old friend from Eton. Lastly there was an old friend of Binky's, Robert, Lord Wingate, the Marquess of Denham's heir."

Garth sat back and looked at the trio. "I don't understand. What have these four gentleman to do with this? Have you questioned the servants?"

Lord Buckleigh drew his hands behind his back. "If you mean do I suspect one of our people, I do not. There's not a one who has been in our employ for less than ten years. They helped inspect the house from top to bottom, and not a single window or door was found unlocked. I did ask about strangers in the house and other than Jack's friends there have been none. I haven't even told them what I suspect about a robbery."

At that moment the door opened and Hickam returned with a cold collation and a tankard of ale. They were all quiet until the butler set the tray on a table. Garth thanked him as he left, then rose and began to pace, ignoring the repast. "Why not call Bow Street?"

Jack snorted. "Did you not hear who we suspect? What chance is there that they will look closely at a titled gentleman or the son of such a man? Short of treason or murder, no peer is ever touched by the crown."

The viscount nodded his agreement. "I cannot even be sure the Runners would mount a proper search for an *objet d'art* in a city full of such treasures. No, we must handle this matter ourselves."

Garth's brows rose. "Sir, what can we do? Surely these gentlemen would all deny having taken the chalice, then we would once again be where we are now."

Jack cleared his throat. "I haven't been standing around idle since this happened. Did some investigating." He looked at his father, who gave him a brief nod, then he continued. "We think we've narrowed it down to the one. He is punting on the River Tick and only he has disappeared from Town since we discovered the theft."

"Which one?" Garth experienced a moment of surprise at the look of maturity that appeared on his brother's face. Whatever else might come of this, Jack would gain some wisdom.

"Denham's heir, Lord Wingate. Hied back to his father's estate in Yorkshire first thing Wednesday morning, or so says the lady from whom he rents rooms. Promised he'd settle his debts once he returned." Jack nodded his head as if that were very telling.

Lady Buckleigh sighed. "I cannot believe that a marquess' son could be so despicable. What shall we do if he has already sold the chalice? Oh, this is dreadful. My nerves are quite shattered."

Garth gave the matter some thought, then shook his head. "I cannot think he would be such a fool. We would be able to follow the trail to him too easily. Unless I miss my guess, he will take the chalice home, remove the jewels and sell them one at a time."

Her ladyship groaned, but her husband patted her shoulder. "Have no fear, dear heart. We shall catch him before he can inflict too much damage on our treasure." The viscount stepped to his heir and put a hand on his shoulder. "Jack and I have come up with a plan, but it mostly involves you since you are not well known in Society circles."

Garth wanted nothing more than to return to the estate and get on with the planting, but this was too important to the family to ignore. "I shall do what must be done, sir. The chalice has meant too much to the good fortune of our family. We don't want to be responsible for its loss. What must I do?"

Lord Buckleigh glanced at his younger son, then back to Garth. "We discussed the options and there is only one sensible course to avoid scandal. You must go to Yorkshire and steal the chalice back from Wingate."

Lord Denham was convinced that luck had forsaken him. His stable hadn't produced a winner in four years despite the expense of bringing in new breeding stock. A letter from his heir had arrived, demanding an increase in his allowance which Robert intended to squander on the tables in London. And just when the marquess thought he'd bred a winner for the next Gold Cup, he received a terse announcement from that Parson creature saying that Lady Rose must be retrieved from Somerset due to the closing of the school. The one thing he didn't need was that chit ripping up his peace again.

There was not the least bit of guilt that three years had slipped by without his once visiting or sending for Lady Rose. He had given little thought to his daughter, being too involved in the pursuit of his own affairs. For men like Denham, daughters were a mere incumbrance.

Never one to distance himself far from his horses and hounds, Lord Denham stirred himself enough to send a terse missive to his son summoning him home. He would insist Robert earn that allowance for once. In the meantime, he would invite the man his solicitor had determined would pay the most for the privilege of Lady Rose's hand.

In London, Lord Wingate, much like his father, had given little thought to his sister over the long years other than to question her absence at table during the first holiday visit to Yorkshire after Rosamund left. The young earl's life was much consumed with the pursuits of the fashionable world of London, especially all matters involving games of chance.

The morning he opened the missive from his father, Robert's head was pounding, and he was fully aware that not one but two men were in possession of his vowels for nearly two thousand pounds after a dreadful night of gaming. He broke the seal, and read not the news he'd hoped—news of a bank draft—but orders to return home at once. He tossed the letter on the table. He bitterly resented his father's demand, but dare not refuse the order for he needed his allowance, pittance that it was. Besides, the races were soon to start in Yorkshire and that was always a way to increase his blunt.

Without delay, Lord Wingate set out that afternoon for home. No sooner had he arrived back at Denham Hall, than the marquess ordered his son to Somerset to bring his sister home, posthaste. Robert fumed about the long journey, but it was not the worst time to be away from London. His outstanding vowels loomed heavily upon him and with no funds to make them good until next quarter day, Somerset was not the worst place to be.

With mixed feelings he set out the following morning to retrieve the troublesome chit. He arrived to find the academy at sixes and sevens with departing females everywhere. Yet his sister was nowhere to be found. Some two hours later in strolled the tardy Lady Rose. This first encounter in three years proved unfortunate. The young lady, returning from a picnic, came upon her brother awaiting her in the foyer. Windblown from her outing, she looked just as she had when she'd departed Yorkshire three years earlier. Deciding his sister had learned nothing in all her time at school, the young lord muttered his thoughts aloud, "Gad, Rosie, I see you are still the sad romp Papa sent away to learn some manners. He ain't going to be well pleased if you still cannot conduct yourself like a proper lady."

His unguarded utterance caused the young lady to depart to her room in a huff. With a shrug of his shoulders, Lord Wingate dismissed his sister from his mind, as a particularly pretty brunette passed him with a coquettish giggle. Moments later the unknown beauty returned to the parlor to ogle the stylish visitor with her friends, keeping Robert well amused while he waited.

Upstairs Lady Rose angrily yanked the black ribbon from her blond hair as she entered the small room she shared with Sarah and Ella. "I'll show him who is a proper lady." The years apart from Robert seemed as nothing to Rose when she remembered his sharp-tongued barbs. As a young girl, she'd trailed behind him, wanting to join in with him and his friends. He'd had no sympathy for her, shouting at her and sending her back home at every opportunity. Furious at his renewed rudeness, she listed all his crimes against her.

Sarah Whiting, trailing behind the fuming Lady Rose, closed the door after Ella entered. The girls went to the small cots and sat down since the space in the attic room was limited and Lady Rose had only minutes to change. Listening to their friend rant against her brother, they exchanged a wary look, for they hadn't seen Rose this out of temper since her first year at school.

In the beginning, Lady Rose's fury was legend and many at school had avoided her, but Sarah and Ella had seen through the girl's angry bluster and befriended her. They soon came to know her independent streak ran deep but she was good-hearted and rarely misbehaved without cause, which even they agreed her father had given her when he sent her to school with only a day's notice.

Hoping to calm her friend, Sarah said, "Don't lose patience with your brother. We *are* rather windblown. It would be easy to mistake our appearance." The trio had spent their last afternoon together in a nearby meadow sharing their fears and dreams for the future now that their school days were at end.

"Would you like me to undo your ties?" Ella asked as Lady Rose continue to pace, making no effort to comply with Robert's demand that she hurry nor Sarah's excuse for his rudeness. "You will be late and gentlemen do so dislike that."

Lady Rose opened her mouth, about to announce she didn't give a fig what he liked or disliked, but seeing the look on her friends' faces she knew she was being childish. Her quarrel with Robert could wait. She pasted a smile on her face, trying to rein in her anger for her friends' sake. "Thank you, Ella. That would be most kind."

Within ten minutes she was dressed in the blue traveling gown in which she'd arrived. The muslin dress had grown tight, especially where she'd grown more womanly. The hem was a bit short showing more ankle than was fashionable, but she reasoned only her father was to blame. She tamed her blond curls into a neat chignon, then donned her only bonnet, a chipstraw with black ribbon. Her small trunk was packed and ready, but she had one last thing she needed to do.

Taking her friends hands, her eyes grew moist. "Do not forget our pact. Should one of us be fortunate enough to find a husband, we shall invite the two others to join them. We have become as family and must not forget one another."

Sarah and Ella, tears glistening in their eyes, hugged Lady Rose and promised. It had been a silly pact they'd made to one another, but the Three Fates knew they each headed home for lives with families who gave little thought to young females without fortunes. They truly had only each other to rely upon.

With a last hug, the three girls trooped downstairs to where Lord Wingate stood looking at his pocket watch, which he closed with an impatient snap. Without further show of temper, the young lady stepped outside to see Dixon, Robert's ever-faithful groom standing holding open the carriage door.

He tugged his slouch hat and grinned at her. "Good to see ye again, my lady."

Lady Rose knew an urge to cry. Why had a mere servant greeted her with more welcome than her own brother? "Dixon, you are looking in good health," she acknowledged. As she approached the groom, she realized that he'd grown from the scrawny youth her brother had rescued from the Watch in a rare moment of drunken benevolence, to a lean giant of nearly six foot.

"I am that, my lady."

Lord Wingate snapped, "Do stop jawing, man and help her in. I want to be in Yorkshire before the Gold Cup is run next week. I have a monkey on Chillingworth's Irish goer."

Within minutes the carriage rumbled down the drive. Lady Rose looked back through the small carriage window at her friends waving goodbye in front of Miss Parson's academy. She would miss them desperately, but there was a part of her that looked forward to being back at Denham Hall. Back to her rides over the moors, her walks in the terraced garden which her mother had so loved, and talks with Chalmers, the family butler, and her old nurse, Benson.

Lord Wingate fell asleep without saying a word to his sister, giving Rose the opportunity to observe her brother undetected. She was surprised at how much he'd changed since last she'd seen him. He was taller and thinner. The lean angular quality to his physique gave him a grown-up appearance. His dark blond hair curled naturally round his face, which she decided one would call handsome. In slumber there was a vulnerability about him that reminded her that his life had been almost as difficult as hers where their father was concerned. Much was expected of him as the heir, and Robert always seemed to disappoint the marquess whether on horseback, in his studies, or in matters of the estate.

Uttering a soft sigh, she realized they should not be at odds with one another. They had a common adversary in their father. She made a vow to try and put their animosity to rest, which she did as soon as he awoke some two hours later.

In a friendly manner, she began to ask him of his life in London. Robert arched one well-shaped eyebrow but answered her questions readily enough. Like most men, he enjoyed speaking of himself. He even loosened up enough to tell her several amusing tales from his early days in Town. "Gad, those were great days."

"Oh, Robert, how I wish I could have come with you instead of being sent to Miss Parson's."

Her brother's brows flattened. "I hope you are not imagining that Papa will allow you to come to London for a Season."

Rose laughed. "I am not such a nodcock. I should be pleased if he will allow me to go to the assemblies in York." Then she looked down at her old traveling gown. "But to own the truth, unless he permits me a few new gowns, I won't even brave those for I should be quite the dowd."

"Good luck," Robert scoffed. "If it weren't for my luck at the tables, I should still be wearing the same suit of clothes I arrived in Town with. All he has ever paid attention to are his cattle, the current race, and fox season."

Rose's gaze swept over her brother's fashionable

gray coat, yellow floral damask waistcoat, and black buckskins. "Have you won a great deal at the tables?"

Robert averted his gaze to the passing scenery. "I win some, I lose some, just like most others."

Sensing this was not a subject to better their relationship, Rose asked if he'd been to see any plays since arriving in Town. Brother and sister spent the remainder of the day in sporadic and generally congenial conversation between long spans of silence. The coach traveled until well after dark, then they spent the night at a dreary inn with poor food and damp beds. Rose did not complain about an early departure the next morning.

By noon the second day, they approached Denham Hall and excitement seemed to build in Rose as the familiar smell of the moors permeated the carriage. She leaned forward in her seat as they crested the top of a hill and the Hall came into view. The gray and honey-colored stonework of the sprawling Jacobean manor was a sharp contrast to the green birches which clustered round the perimeter of the gardens. The house and gardens were like a billowing oasis set down in the stark moors, but Rose loved the very sight of the place.

"Put me down at the garden gate," she demanded.

Robert tapped the roof and called for the coachman to stop out front. "I shall go to the stables with the carriage. I want to see the new spring foals. Not that Papa would ever allow me to manage one of them." The bitterness in his voice was at odds with the benign expression on his face.

Nothing was going to spoil her first day back. Without waiting for Dixon, she opened the door and flipped down the steps. She descended and entered the gate without a backward glance. The sound of the carriage moving away barely penetrated her delight at being once again in the garden that she'd helped her mother plan. Pulling the bonnet from her head, she freed her hair from the restrictive chignon, basking in the delightful May sunshine and warm afternoon breeze. For nearly an hour she wandered about among the colorful array of blooms, lost in remembering the long afternoons laughing with her mother as they instructed the gardener where to put the various plants to form just the right effect.

To Rose's disappointment, the gardens had clearly suffered neglect. The flower beds were full of weeds, the shrubs were unclipped. In the distance she could see that the gazebo near the ornamental lake needed paint. Yet even in its unruly splendor, the gardens still owned a natural charm. With hard work and one good gardener she could bring it back to its former glory. She suspected that all the hard work might be hers for her father had reduced the gardening staff after the death of her mother.

After strolling from one end of the gardens to the other, she decided she must face her father. She followed the path that led to the front of the house. Her mother was gone, but Chalmers and Benson would be happy to see her even if her father wasn't. She reached out for the front door handle but the oaken panel swept opened before her fingers could touch the tarnished brass lever.

She gasped at the sight of the most handsome man she'd ever seen. He stood gazing at her as bemused by her appearance as she was by his. The blue of his deep-set eyes seemed to pierce her very soul and she stood mute, wondering who he might be, and why was he at Denham?

In a rich husky voice, he asked, "May I help you?"

It took several minutes for her to realize what he had said, so stunned was she by his handsome looks. "Who are you?"

"Sterling, miss, the new butler."

Rose stepped back and for the first time took in his drab, black attire which held not the least hint of fashion, despite the athletic physique beneath. "B-but how can this be? Butlers are old and gray and portly, like Chalmers." They did not have broad shoulders and chest. They did not have piercing blue eyes and shiny black hair. They did not make one's very toes curl.

A smile played at the corner of the man's well-shaped mouth. "I do believe given enough time I could acquire those things you find essential, but I assure you I am quite capable in my present condition."

A blush burned Rose's cheeks. "Where is Chalmers?"

"Gone." The man's face was once again a mask of polite interest.

It had never occurred to Rose that her dear Chalmers would be gone. He was as much a part of her life here at Denham as Robert and her father. He had been the one to administer to her during any childhood mishap, to protect her from her father's wrath, to comfort her after her mother's death, to urge her to bend to her father's will, to tell her she would survive her life at school and be the better for it. She was sure her heart would break that the gentle old man would no longer be there to chide her for her misdeeds, to dry her tears, and cheer her successes. She hadn't even been able to say her goodbyes.

Worse, her father had managed to hire a man who looked like he should be escorting her to a ball, not bringing her cocoa or retrieving coats and hats. She suddenly realized Sterling was staring at her with a twinkle of amusement in those amazing eyes. Who did he think he was to be laughing at her? She straightened her shoulders and with as much dignity as she could muster in her ill-fitting old traveling gown with her hair flying loose in the breeze, she asked, "Where is my father?"

A startled look sobered the young butler. "You are Lady Rosamund? Is Lord Wingate with you?" He gazed past her, a searching look in his eyes as if he were disappointed that she was alone.

"I *am* Lady Rose and my brother has gone to the stables." She stepped into the great hall, looking about to see what other changes had been wrought in her absence, but all seemed to be as it was. Then her gaze locked on the portrait of her beautiful mother and her throat tightened. The Hall seemed so cold and empty without her mother. Rose started when the butler spoke.

"His lordship is gone to York with friends, my lady. Shall I show you to your room so that you might freshen up before your father returns?" His gaze roved to the blond tendrils which curled about her shoulders in disarray.

Seeing his censoring inspection, again Rose's cheeks warmed. She needed to look her best when she met her father but she hated the fact that the new butler was the one to remind her of that. Still, she was determined to be on her best behavior, so she said, "There is no need, Sterling, I am quite sure I can find my way."

With that she marched up the main staircase, resisting the urge to look back at the man who was a young girl's image of Prince Charming. But he was a servant and she must remember to keep her distance from such a man.

Madness! Garth knew of no other way to describe what he was doing here in Yorkshire. He'd told his father and brother just that when they'd explained their plan. He'd informed Hickam of the same thing as the old man had gone over and over the rules of behavior for a proper butler. Yet here he was at Denham Hall trying to convince everyone he was a butler.

He still didn't know what his father had done with the marquess' former butler. It was only after the Marquess of Denham grudgingly hired him that Garth learned that as far as everyone at the Hall knew, the old man had simply disappeared one day. A few days later a letter had arrived informing Lord Denham that Chalmers had inherited a small legacy and wouldn't be returning.

The position had been a close thing, for Lord Denham had expressed doubts about hiring someone so young. Only the glowing letter from Lord Melbourne had done the trick and Garth's willingness to work for such paltry wages as the marquess offered.

Over the past week, he had developed a great deal of respect for the unknown Chalmers. The old man had coped with the vagaries of Lord Denham's temper, almost no staff to maintain this enormous manor, and even less money to manage the household expenses. The frustrating fact was, there had been no time for Garth to search for the chalice. That didn't concern him overmuch since, according to Thomas, the lone footman, Lord Wingate had scarcely taken his hat off before his father sent him off to Somerset.

Garth closed the front door of the Hall. So, the suspected thief was home at last. Did he have the Chalice of Naples with him, was the question. No doubt he'd had little time to do anything with the goblet and still carried it in his luggage. But now that he was at the estate, one thing was for certain, there were a thousand and one places to hide the cup in the manor or on the grounds, which only made Garth's job harder. He would have to keep watch over the young man, as much as his duties would allow.

To his surprise, his thoughts veered to Wingate's lovely sister. Despite the urgency of his mission, his reveries dwelled on Lady Rosamund whose existence he'd only learned about from Cook that very morning. The tales of her antics had amused him. She would have been a thorn in the side of the self-absorbed Denham.

The young lady made a striking appearance, but she was scarcely out of the schoolroom. Having resided in the same household with the boorish marquess for the past week, the female he'd just encountered was something of a surprise to Garth. True, she'd been dressed in an outmoded gown which was too small and her hair was unkempt, but there had been an elegance about her that had shown through her *farouche* appearance. His gaze roved up the stairs where the young lady had disappeared.

His thoughts lingered on her wide kissable mouth and when she'd grown angry with him—her green eyes had flashed fire—an intriguing little minx and one who was out of bounds. Not that he was interested in pursuing the chit anyway. He didn't envy the fellow that would have Denham as a father-in-law.

"Sterling!" Lord Denham's voice roared from the library. "Damme, where is that fellow? You cannot get good help in England since all the best lads dashed off to fight the French!"

Garth rolled his eyes. The man was a boor of the first order. Tugging at the plain black waistcoat, Garth made his way to the library, schooling his features to just the proper servile quality that Hickam had taught him.

The marquess, as was his usual practice when coming from the stables, had entered the library from a door that led from the gardens, accompanied by his pack of spotted hounds who presently jostled one another for a position on the rug in front of the fire. Today Denham was not alone. Garth eyed the second gentleman warily, for the danger of being recognized was never far from his mind. The middle-aged man was splendidly dressed in a well-cut blue coat with a black and yellow waistcoat over dark blue buckskins. His Hessians were polished to a shine that would make even the most meticulous dandy in Town proud. He puffed on a cigar as he inspected a painting on the wall, absentmindedly straightening his cravat. He appeared to be in his late forties or early fifties, but the ravages of a dissipated life had marred a once handsome face, making it difficult to judge. Rather puffy eyes and a large paunch diminished the effect of his expensive wardrobe. Dismissing the gentleman as just another one of the marquess' raffish friends with whom he was not acquainted, Garth stepped into his role.

"You wished to see me, my lord."

"There you are at last, Sterling. I warned you, no dawdling when I summon you," the marquess grumbled. Then he turned and gestured to his guest. "The

Earl of Cherrington has just arrived from Carlisle. Bring us my best brandy then prepare rooms for him. He is to stay for the week and join us at the races."

"Very good, my lord."

Garth turned to leave the room, but before he could close the door, he overheard the visitor ask, "When can I meet this lovely daughter I've heard so much about?"

A low chuckle emanated from the marquess, "Ah, an eager swain. I like that."

A wave of distaste washed over Garth when he realized the gentleman was intended for Lady Rosamund. An image of the lively young woman rose before him and Garth chuckled softly. He suspected that the lady would have none of old Cherrington, despite his fashionable clothes and title.

As he made his way downstairs an idea popped into the faux butler's head. Perhaps he just might give the young lady a helping hand in ridding herself of so distasteful a suitor. A fiendish twinkle was in his eye as he sent Meg to prepare the Gold Bedroom in which the chimney smoked when the wind was from the east. Without hesitation he ordered James to the cellar for the plum brandy instead of the good French kegs, and he informed Cook there would be three new places at dinner but the usual fare of mutton and potatoes would do for the night.

That done, Garth returned to his office just off the kitchen and the job of determining what household duties were needing attention. Once he returned to Hillcrest, Garth intended to give Hickam a substantial increase in salary. Of one thing he was certain, a butler's work seemed never to be done.

* * *

"Father must have done something dreadful to make Chalmers leave in such a manner. Why, this Sterling fellow looks hardly old enough to be head footman, much less butler." Rose paced back and forth in front of her old nurse, Benson. The woman was thin and wiry with slate gray hair and faded brown eyes, yet her face held a gentleness that belied the hardships of her life. Despite that, Rose well knew that beneath the soft countenance was a woman of principle who did her duty regardless of the consequences.

At present, Rose's thoughts still lingered on the changes at the manor, as she sat in her room these past two hours. She was uncertain which bothered her most, Chalmers's strange departure or Sterling's well-featured presence.

After snipping the thread, Nurse put down the needle she used to mend the linens long past their prime. It was a thankless task, but necessary.

"For once child, I cannot agree with you. The letter clearly stated Mr. Chalmers inherited a legacy. There was no need for him to wait to be pensioned off, not that your father would have done so. As to Sterling, I feel him far too young and handsome for such a position, but his lordship has never seen fit to ask my opinion about anything." Years as a faithful servant with great affection allowed Rose's old nurse to speak the truth where the marquess was concerned. None could remember when a servant had been sent into retirement with a livable income.

Rose stopped her pacing and stared at the woman. A guilty flush settled on her cheeks. She stepped forward and took the old woman's hands. "I promise, I shall see that you are given a pension and sent to live wherever you should like as soon as I may."

Benson smiled and patted her former charge's hand. "That is most kind of you, child. But I could never leave Denham Hall until you are safely married and"—there was the implied thought "safe from your father's neglect"—but the woman finished with, "And, well, there is no point in spinning dreams that the marquess will present you as he should."

The servant folded the sheet she'd been darning, then stopped, a hopeful expression on her lined countenance. "By chance did you meet someone who touched your heart while you were away, my dear?"

The face of Sterling sprang into Rose's mind so suddenly she protested angrily. "Of course not, Benny. I have been locked in the wilds of Somerset, not going to fashionable parties."

The old woman rose, putting aside her work. "Well, at least here you shall have your old amusements, but promise me you will not be up to any of your old tricks."

Rose had learned her lesson; there would be no question of that. "I promise."

A knock sounded at the door and a strange breathlessness seemed to overtake Rose at the prospect of who might be at her door. Meg, one of the upstairs maids, stuck her head inside the door, deflating all expectations in the young lady. "Beggin' your pardon, my lady, but his lordship says as you're to put on your best gown for this evenin' since he's entertaining."

A frown puckered Rose's smooth brow. "Who is dining with us?"

"The Earl of Cherrington, my lady." With that the girl closed the door.

Rose turned to Benson who shrugged. "Don't ask me, child. I've never met the gentleman. I suspect he is here for the races or to purchase one of your father's horses. My question to you would be, have you anything decent to wear this evening?"

Rose shook her head.

"Then we must put our heads together child, for one never knows who might come to call during the races." Benson winked at Rose who grinned at the prospect of meeting a handsome young lord at her father's table. One who would quite supplant her fascination with Sterling, which was indeed quite shocking.

The two women spent the remainder of the afternoon trying to find a proper evening gown for Lady Rosamund. The girl's wardrobe from school consisted of three gray dresses, the blue traveling gown, which clearly was too small, and a worn white muslin day dress that Rose wore to church on Sundays. Of the garments she had left behind, none fit properly. As a last resort, they went to Lady Denham's rooms and found a simple blue silk evening dress with tiny pearls worked into the bodice which Benson was able to alter in time for Rose to dress before the gong sounded for dinner.

At six sharp, Rose was startled as she stepped to the mirror in her room. Benson had done wonders with the dress and with Rose's hair. The blue watered silk seemed to shimmer in the light. They'd taken a strip of excess silk to create a simple band to hold up the golden curls that Nurse had drawn into a topknot. A cluster of loose curls were allowed to dangle in the back. Rose was delighted. She looked a proper, presentable young lady. "Oh, you are a miracle worker, Benny."

The older woman merely smiled with pride from her chair in the corner. "You look much like your mama did in that gown, child. Enjoy your evening."

When Rose made her way down to the drawing room, she was once again struck with how much she sorely missed Chalmers. Were he here she could have questioned him about their guest. The thought of befriending Sterling in such a manner was not to be considered.

At that moment, the man she'd been thinking of stepped from the drawing room. Rose thought a hint of admiration flashed in his eyes before it was gone, replaced by a stony aloofness. "His lordship is waiting, Lady Rosamund."

The butler held the door open for her, and Lady Rose stepped into the drawing room, strangely aware of the man at her side. Why did her father replace dear old Chalmers with a young handsome man? That thought was pushed from her mind as her gaze swept Lord Cherrington who stood beside her father and brother in all his fleshy splendor. She sighed heavily with disappointment. For a moment she thought she heard the whispered words, "Fear not." But when her gaze flashed to Sterling's face, there was no hint he'd spoken, only a mask of polite servitude. He then closed the door, leaving her feeling quite alone despite her companions.

To her disappointment the earl was old and round and far too loud as he spoke with her father. But she knew she must be on her best behavior. She was determined to show her parent that she could conduct herself like a proper lady. "Good evening, Father, Wingate. Lord Cherrington, welcome to Denham Hall."

Two

Near dawn the next morning, Rose peered stealthily out her bedroom door. Seeing not a soul in the darkened hall, she left her room and made her way to the main stairs. A lone candle lit her way as she gripped the tail of her habit so she would not trip as she tiptoed along the worn carpet. Her faded green garment was her only option if she wished to ride, for her mother had not been a horsewoman, to her husband's dismay. Like her traveling gown, the habit had grown a bit tight, but Rose was determined to ride this morning and without the company of Lord Cherrington.

A shudder raced down her spine as memories of last night's supper filled her mind. The old earl had taken to gazing at her in a way that frightened her. He'd droned on and on about Cherring Chase, his estate in Carlisle. In an effort to please her father she'd asked several polite questions, but she experienced a feeling of distaste when his gaze moved over her in the most leering manner as if he were afraid he might miss some small detail of her person. On several occasions he'd taken her hand to put a wet lingering kiss upon her skin. Even Robert raised his brows at such an intimacy.

Her father had made matters worse by sitting

there smirking at her like a cat at the cream pot. Still, the only time she seemed to displease the marquess had been when she begged off from riding with Cherrington. She'd pleaded fatigue from her journey North. Even to gratify her parent she would not share her first ride across the moors with anyone save the mandatory groom, which she had quite resigned herself to accept.

The main hall stood empty as she halted at the foot of the stairs to listen for movement by the servants. The house lay quiet, but that did not mean the kitchen was not busy. She had learned long ago that noises from below stairs did not reach the front hall. She hurried across the black and white marble floor to the front door, then set her candle on a nearby table. Had her father kept her favorite mare, Vesta? She grasped the door handle and pressed down on the lever, only to discover the portal was locked. She quickly searched the nearby tables but the key was nowhere to be found. The new butler either had hidden the key or kept it on him. Had her father warned him of her youthful escapades? She felt like shouting to the top of her lungs that she would not be treated like some disobedient child who needed constant supervision. But if she'd learned one thing in the last three years, it was that tantrums did not gain one what one wished for. Were a few hours of freedom too much to desire?

Rose nipped at her lip a moment, pondering how she might slip out of the house without anyone seeing her. Going through the kitchens would be out of the question. It would be disaster if one of the servants were to inform her father she had ridden this morning after refusing his friend. There had to be another way out. She hurried to the long doors in the front drawing room but they, also, were locked. In fact all the doors she found to be locked as she made her way from the formal drawing rooms to the family parlors in the rear of the house.

Through the windows of the Green Parlor she could see the sun's rays brightening the eastern sky. If she didn't hurry, she would miss her opportunity to ride that day. If she rode in the afternoon, there would be no escaping unwanted company. In a moment of desperation, she blew out her candle, then stepped to one of the windows and undid the latch. She pushed open the framed diamond-shaped panes and stared at the ground below. It seemed a long way down, but she was certain she could safely make the jump.

With a quick look around the room she found a chair the right height and dragged it to the window. She stepped onto the needlepoint cushion, then up to the windowsill. The opening was narrow and she shifted her weight to be able to slip through. As she was about to step to the ledge outside, a voice startled her.

"May I help you, Lady Rose?"

To Rose's horror, Sterling stood not ten feet from her. He was neatly dressed in his butler's black, his simple white cravat the only relief from the austere hue. While his face revealed nothing of his thoughts, his eyes twinkled. Why did he always seemed to be amused by her *gaffes*?

Her cheeks burned, and she didn't know what to say being caught in such a position. "I . . . er . . .that is . . ."

"You were going for some morning air, my lady?"

There was no point in pretending she wasn't climbing out the window. "The house was locked and I wished to be early at the stables."

"Afraid all the good mounts would be gone before you arrived?" His mouth twitched, and it was obvious that he knew that the marquess kept well over thirty horses at any one time.

Rose couldn't help but grin. "Of course not, but I did wish to ride on my first morning back and well— I wanted to be alone."

"You have no need to explain, my lady." The butler stepped to her, and offered his hand. "Allow me."

Rose hesitated a moment, then took the proffered help. A strange tingle seemed to race up her arm as he helped her to the floor, but she attributed it to her great embarrassment at having been caught climbing out the window.

Once back on the floor, she eyed him warily. "You won't tell my father, will you?"

Sterling pulled the window shut and locked the hasp. "Tell him what, Lady Rose? That one of the servants carelessly left a window open?" A hint of a smile touched his handsome mouth, then his face settled back to expressionlessness. "If that is all, I must go and unlock the front door in case someone wants to take an early ride."

She smiled and followed behind him, grateful for his kindness. For the first time since she'd returned home, she realized that despite his youthful age, he might be an ally just as Chalmers had been. She watched him take long, lithe strides, and couldn't help but notice he had physical assets she had never dreamed of looking for on Chalmers.

La! She'd better keep her mind from wondering along that track. Although he was exceptionally handsome, he was still a butler, not a gentleman. She would simply have to remind herself that young ladies of Quality did not think romantic thoughts about servants no matter how good their looks.

After the lock was undone, he opened the door for her. "Thank you, Sterling." She swept through the door, then paused on the front stoop to take in the wonderful sight of her beloved Yorkshire that she'd so missed.

"Enjoy your day, my lady."

The door closed behind her. She turned and stared at it a moment. There was no justice that the only man nearby who could make a young lady sigh was not a suitable prospect. But then as Rose had learned in the past three years, there was little in life that was fair.

The crow of a rooster in the distance reminded her that time was slipping by and she could not afford to waste a minute. Lifting the hem of her old green habit, she made a mad dash for the stables.

Luck was with her that morning and only her old friend, Padgett, one of the under grooms, was busy at his post. He had begun the early morning feeding and watering of her father's cattle. With funds so limited, the stable staff was still well below normal, but that seemed to be the perpetual state of things at the Hall. The Marquess of Denham was known for breeding the best Arabians in Yorkshire, but with only one or two top-flight foals a season due to the vagaries of breeding, money remained tight. Especially when the marquess often wagered his blunt on the wrong racer. If only he might stay with breeding horses and not wagering on them, Denham Hall might once again be prosperous.

On spying Lady Rose striding toward the stable, Padgett tugged his hat from his head, then smoothed his wispy brown curls with his hand. "My lady, I heard ye was back and wondered when ye was comin' down to see Vesta."

"My father hasn't sold her? What a relief." Rose followed the groom down the aisle of the mare's keep and on the end she found her favorite mount. The sleek little dappled Arabian poked her head out beyond the rope enclosure and snorted, seeming to remember her. Rose stroked the mare's nose as the animal snorted her approval.

"Is she breeding or can I take her out, Paddy?"

"She didn't take this spring, my lady." The groom eyed Lady Rose thoughtfully. "If ye is willin' to take young Will with ye, yer welcome to ride her. Otherwise, ye can't. I done had enough flesh taken off me back by your Da's tongue to know ye can't be gallopin' about the countryside alone."

Excitement fluttered in Rose's chest. It seemed like an eternity since she'd last ridden. Miss Parson never kept horses at the academy, her excuse being the danger to the girls, but Rose thought it was more the expense. "I shall take whomever you say, but you mustn't tell my father I rode this morning, nor Lord Cherrington."

A frown puckered Padgett's bushy brows. "Yer father ain't like to ask and I ain't tellin' that nick-ninny earl naught. Can't trust a man what drives the finest carriage money can buy with the washiest bits of blood I ever seen."

A laugh bubbled up inside Rose. It had only taken Paddy one look to take the earl's measure. What did her father see in a man who couldn't distinguish looks from substance in horseflesh? She supposed gentlemen often disregarded such deficiencies when a title was involved.

Some ten minutes later she sat comfortably on

Vesta, heading for the moors with young Will who struggled to keep on her trail. Perhaps things would not be so very awful now that she was back at home. Once Cherrington departed, life might well get back to how it had been before she had been sent away to school.

Garth, standing at the front window, watched with amusement as the young lady lifted her skirts and dashed towards the stables. She was a strange mix of woman and child, and certainly not ready for the likes of Cherrington. Thoughts of the earl possessing Lady Rose sent a strange rush of anger coursing through Garth's veins. He'd seen the old man fawning over the girl at dinner and later while serving tea in the drawing room. She had done an excellent job of masking her distaste, still, Garth had sensed her withdrawal each time the earl had approached. Garth wished he knew some way to help her foil her father's plans to wed her to such a man.

By Jove, Garth swore under his breath, what was wrong with him? It was common practice for families to marry their daughters to wealthy and titled older men. So why did the thought of Lady Rose's possible betrothal bother him so much? He hardly knew the young lady and he had other pressing matters at hand. He'd scarcely had a moment to search for the chalice since Wingate arrived.

Pushing the girl's problems from his mind, Garth pondered where he should begin. In Wingate's bedroom, without a doubt, but the Town Tulip was not likely to be out of bed before noon. That would give Garth time to take care of his morning duties until

Meg informed him she was finished with the bed-chambers.

He went to the library and set the fire, knowing it would take some time to remove the chill from the room and Thomas was busy helping Cook in the kitchen. About to depart, Garth moved to the windows that faced the East and peered out at the brightening day. He caught the sight of a dapple gray horse with rider cantering down the front drive, a young groom frantically trying to keep pace. As she distanced herself from the house, Lady Rose effortlessly moved the horse into a full gallop. Within minutes she was out the front gate and dashing over the moors to the top of the nearest hill. She exhibited an excellent seat and he experienced a sudden burst of envy. How he wished he were racing across the moors beside Lady Rose instead of worrying about the ongoing battle between Meg and Thomas over who sat where at table each morning. Or worrying whether the ham and eggs on the sideboard were still warm when the marquess and his guests served themselves. Or praying he might find the time to search for his family's chalice.

As the young lady disappeared over the hill, the thought of her with a man like Cherrington set Garth's teeth on edge. He turned away from the window.

Drat it! He had no business involving himself in Lady Rose's life. His focus must remain on finding the Chalice of Naples. A smile tipped his mouth. Well, if the occasional opportunity to secretly needle the Earl of Cherrington arose, he would not pass it by. Such simple pleasures did not hinder his mission in the least. On that thought he made his way back downstairs until the remainder of the family awoke.

* * *

Some two hours later Lady Rose, back in her room, donned another one of her mother's dresses that Benson had altered overnight. The deep pink and white striped muslin with solid pink bodice worked with white ribbon brought the roses out in the young lady's cheeks. A knock sounded on Rose's bedroom door as she admired Benny's skilled needlework. Meg poked her head in when summoned. "My lady, your father wishes to see you in the library at two this afternoon. He says not to be late."

"I shall be there." She smiled at Meg, then after the servant departed wondered what her father might have to say to her. Despite her distaste for Cherrington, she'd been on her best behavior. Would he reprimand her for not riding with his friend?

After she brushed out the tangles and re-pinned her chignon, Rose sought out Benson and questioned her about the meeting. But the old woman, ensconced in the sewing room with a bundle of Lady Denham's old gowns, did not know why his lordship wanted to see her. The women whiled away the remainder of the morning in idle conversation about what had been happening in the neighborhood since Rose had left. Many of her childhood friends and acquaintances were either gone off to war and not yet returned with the peace or were gone to London and married. She tried not to dwell too much on the fact that she would have no Season like most of her childhood friends. Instead, if her father were in a good mood, she might beg permission to attend the assemblies in York. Benny's talented fingers and her mother's old wardrobe would make her presentable without the least expense to her father's already depleted finances.

At precisely two that afternoon Rose knocked on the door of the library. When she heard her father's voice, she entered and found him sitting in front of the fireplace, a glass of brandy in his hand. He raked her with his hard gaze before saying, "Come, girl, sit down. We have important matters to discuss."

His very tone sent a chill down Rose's spine. What could they have to discuss? She had only just returned home and done nothing to raise him to a fit of anger. She perched herself on the edge of the black leather wing chair which faced him, not feeling comfortable enough under her father's merciless stare to relax against the cushions.

The marquess put his glass aside then crossed his arms. "I must say that old dragon Parson was worth every penny I paid. You look quite the proper female."

Rose blushed as her father swept her with a thoughtful gaze. Did he see the resemblance to her mother that Benny saw? She wasn't certain that was such a good thing, because her parents' relationship had often been strained and acrimonious. Yet Rose could not deny that her mother had been beautiful and she deemed it a compliment that anyone would think her close to the beauty of Lady Denham. Rose remained silent as her father continued to stare at her in an assessing manner.

For the first time since returning home she took a good long look at him. Time and excesses were starting to take their toll on a man who never could have been called handsome. His reddish blond hair had grown sparse on top, and his mustache flecked with gray. The leathery skin about his eyes and mouth crinkled in radiating lines even when he wasn't smiling, not that he smiled often in Rose's company. His worn riding coat strained at the buttons over a paunch he'd developed, and his hands were looking a bit gnarled, more like a farmer's than a gentleman's.

As the silence lengthened, she grew uneasy. Very often in the past she'd only been summoned to be reprimanded, but she'd done nothing. Impatient to know what he intended, she asked, "What did you wish to see me about, Father?"

He seemed to start from his brown study, and barked, "How old are you, girl?"

"Soon to be twenty, sir."

He nodded his head. "Past time you were married."

Rose's eyes widened. "But I am not yet out, nor have I . . ."

"No need for that waste of money. As your father, I shall handle such matters, for one should never leave important financial dealing to the whims of a girl's heart."

Fear gripped at Rose and her hands trembled. What did her father have in mind? Then it dawned on her why her father had invited a man like Cherrington to Denham. "Sir, surely you would not ask me to marry where I do not love?"

A satisfied grin stretched the marquess' mouth. "Ask, girl? Not likely. I am telling you that Lord Cherrington intends to make you his bride."

All Rose's determination to be on her best behavior flew out the window at that pronouncement. She bounded to her feet. "I have only just returned home, sir. I do not wish to be married." Seeing the black look come into her father's green eyes, Rose tried to temper her defiance. "Please do not think I am ungrateful for your efforts on my behalf, but I cannot marry the Earl of Cherrington."

Her father rose to face her, his countenance growing bright red with outrage. "You will do as you are told, girl. The earl is as rich as Golden Ball and the funds in the settlement are very generous for us both."

Cherrington! The very thought of the man as her husband made Rose shudder. All the subservience of her three years at school fell away. Marriage was too important to her future to allow herself be led to the altar like a sheep. But she feared she might say something which she would regret. Thinking she would do better to make her declaration and leave, she strode to the door of the library, yanked it open then looked back at her father. "I will not marry the earl, sir, not now or ever." She turned and left the room.

Lord Denham moved with a speed that belied his size and years. He arrived at his daughter's side before she'd taken two steps into the hallway. He grabbed her arm and spun her round, then drew back his hand and struck her across the cheek. The stinging blow sent her hurtling backward. Unprepared for the violent assault, she lost her balance and fell to the floor. Appalled, she stared up at her father in horror as her hand came up to cover the tingling skin on her cheek.

The blow echoed strangely in the great hall and the sound of footsteps advancing caused both father and daughter to look up as the butler made his way to them with dark eyes glittering at the marquess.

"Stay where you are Sterling, if you value your job," Lord Denham growled as he pointed at the servant.

Warring emotions played on the servant's face, then he straightened, and stared at the marquess in that expressionless way of all servants. Still he did not leave.

Lord Denham turned his wrath back to his daughter. "I will hear no more of this nonsense. The banns

will be read on Sunday and you will marry Cherrington three weeks hence." He looked from his
daughter to the butler. "Sterling, escort Lady Rose to
her room where she is to remain for the rest of the
day. As for you girl, when you come down for supper
be prepared to accept the earl's offer of marriage.
You will regret any other decision."

With that the gentleman strode back into his library and slammed the door shut.

Rose closed her eyes and fought back tears. In all
her days at the academy she could never have imagined her father would do this on her return.

Three

A black rage consumed Garth as he glared at the Marquess of Denham towering over his daughter where she lay on the floor. What kind of beast was the man? How could he strike his own child in such a heartless manner? It took all Garth could muster not to plant the man a facer, but Lady Rose appeared more startled than truly harmed. He reminded himself that it was his duty to keep pursuing his family's chalice, not to be drawn into the Dennison family's conflicts.

After Lord Denham made a final threat to his daughter, he turned on his heel and disappeared into his library. Garth sprang into action. He knelt beside the young lady and was forced to tamp down an urge to take her in his arms to comfort her. At this moment his role as family butler greatly inhibited what he could do to give her aid. Her eyes were closed and her breathing a bit ragged, a hand covering her cheek. He stayed his bounds and merely asked, "Are you unharmed, my lady?"

Her green eyes opened and revealed all the pain of that moment. Words seemed to be beyond her as she nodded her head, and she dropped her hand, revealing the red welt. Her gaze roved about the room as if she had suddenly found herself in some world that was unfamiliar. There could be little doubt that even she had never expected her father to behave so viciously.

"Allow me to help you to your room, my lady." Garth assisted her to her feet. She took a deep breath as if steeling herself to face the horror of the life her father had planned for her.

"That won't be necessary, Sterling." A wan smile touched her lips. She stood in silence at last grasping all that had just occurred, then after a few moments she seemed to regain her mettle. Her head rose and a smoldering look ignited her countenance.

She spoke more to herself than to him when she announced, "I am not so easily defeated, as my father will soon learn."

Was she trying to convince herself? he wondered.

He stepped back, his brows puckered with worry. He had little doubt that the marquess would be ruthless when crossed. Did she? Garth knew in his role he should keep his own counsel, but he could not let her strike back in anger with little heed for the consequences. "Be careful, my lady. Your father is a desperate man. From what I have seen, this estate is at the brink of financial ruin and your advantageous marriage is his salvation."

Her gaze flew to him, a thoughtful expression transformed her lovely face. Had he overstepped his role? No true butler would intrude with advice even in the worst of situations, especially one newly hired.

Without a word, she turned and went to the foot of the stairs. Pausing, she looked back at him. "I am a desperate *woman*, Sterling. I would rather be dead than married to Lord Cherrington."

Her words hung in the air as she hurried up the stairs, then disappeared from sight at the landing.

Garth's stomach twisted with alarm. What did she mean? Would she try to harm herself? The thought spurred him to dart up the stairs after her. He overtook her halfway down the long carpeted hall and planted himself in her path. "My lady, what are you planning?"

Lady Rose halted, seemingly bewildered by his appearance in front of her. "Planning? As yet nothing, but I shall not willingly accept this marriage."

He wouldn't risk being tactful, this was too important. "You do not intend to harm yourself?"

"Harm myself? Good heavens, no." Her eyes widened. "You thought I meant to . . . ?" She gave a bitter laugh. "When you know me better, Sterling, you will realize that it is other people's welfare you should be concerned about when I am angry, not my own." She gave him a grim smile, then continued past him down the hall. A minute later the door to her room clicked shut behind her.

A half-smile tipped his mouth. She was certainly pluck to the backbone. But would that be enough to withstand her father's strong will? Could she save herself from this arranged marriage? It was an unfortunate fact that females had little control over their lives.

Garth shook his head in frustration. This tempest between Lord Denham and his daughter would only complicate his life. He was here for his family, but should he sacrifice finding the Chalice of Naples to protect Lady Rose from her father's wrath? Perhaps Denham had done his worst. Garth rubbed his neck to relieve his fatigue while he pondered his dilemma. He would have to deal with any further altercations should they arise. He didn't think he could stand idly by if the gentleman struck Lady Rose again.

He stared at her closed door and tried to decide what best to do next. She was safe in her room for the present, but he would stay vigilant. If she openly defied her father again she could be in danger of more physical abuse. Circumstances might well come to a head this evening. That appeared to be the designated time for Lord Cherrington's proposal. There was little Garth needed to do to protect her until then.

With little time to waste, he departed the hall with a determined step. The household duties needed to be overseen before the evening meal. He hoped, if he were lucky, he might get at least one chance to search for the chalice before the coming clash of wills between the Dennisons.

Rose wept in Benson's arms with an abandon which she hadn't known since her mother's death. She had put on a brave face for Sterling, but in truth she was in despair. Her father wanted this marriage, and there were few options for a penniless female but to do as she was bid. That or to run away like some heroine in one of those penny novels that the girls used to read at school. But she had nowhere to go and no money. The utter hopelessness of it all bore down on her once she'd poured her heart out to her old nurse.

"There, there, my dear," Benson stroked Rose's hair as the young lady sat with her head in the old woman's lap. "Perhaps it won't be so bad being the wife of a wealthy earl."

Through sniffles, Rose said, "But I do not wish to marry, and especially not an old man. Why can I not stay here as I did before? I require no great expense.

I won't even pester Father to allow me to go to York to the assemblies should he allow me to stay."

Benson sighed. "My dear child, you are not the first young lady in England asked to marry for money and position. It is the way things are done and has been for centuries."

Rose lifted her head. "But what about love, Benny?"

The old woman gently took her young charge's head between her hands. "You are grown, my lady. Life is not one of those fairy tales I used to read to you. One does one's duty to family. Given time you might learn to love Lord Cherrington."

Rose bounded to her feet. "I do not think so. I should far rather run away and starve in some field than face such a future."

Benson stilled her fright at Lady Rose's announcement. Few who knew the young lady would doubt that she was brave enough to attempt such a dangerous act. She'd been scarcely ten years old when she'd ridden to York alone to buy ribbons for her mother. Ribbons which her father had forbade the lady to buy. The child had more courage than was safe for a female, in Nurse's opinion.

"You are speaking foolishly, my dear. Promise me you will do nothing rash until you fully consider all the consequences. Remember, your mother did her duty."

"And look how that turned out. Father wasted every cent of her money and made her life miserable much of the time." Rose moved to the window and stared out, seeing not the green hills but a bleak future.

"But her ladyship would never have changed a thing once she had her children."

That quieted Rose. Of one thing she had been certain, her mother had loved and protected her.

Would she feel the same about any child of her own no matter who the father was?

Nurse, seeing a softening in Rose's defiance, offered, "Why not go for a ride and calm yourself? That always seems to help you think more clearly. Remember child, fashionable wives rarely see their husbands. You would have money, position, and as many horses as his lordship could buy."

The list of possible advantages didn't appear to sway Rose into capitulating to her father's wishes. The ride however did appeal to her. She looked out at the dark clouds at the horizon. She could ride for at least an hour before the storm ruined the day. But her day was already ruined so what did a few rain drops matter? She eyed Nurse thoughtfully before she said, "And what if I still decide that running away is my only option?"

The old woman plucked nervously at her worn shawl before she lifted her gaze to the child she loved so dearly. "Then, my dear, there will be no other course but that I must accompany you. But you must promise me that you will think fully on this decision. Leaving Denham Hall will likely ruin you and your father would cast us off forever."

Rose took a deep breath. She knew what it had cost Benson to promise to go with her. There would be no safe place for the old woman to live out her retirement. Rose stepped forward and took Benson's hands. "I promise I shall make no rash decision to leave. I am fully aware of the dangers involved in such a scheme. Pray, send Meg to the stables and ask Paddy to have Vesta saddled and at the White Arbor in ten minutes. Tell him not to let anyone know I intend to ride except the groom."

Benson rose and the two women stared at one

another for a brief moment, knowing that Rose held both their fates in her hands. After Nurse departed, Rose went to the wardrobe and pulled out her riding habit. The next hour she had a great deal to consider, for it wouldn't just be her life she was ruining but Benny's as well.

Some ten minutes later the young lady slipped out the front door of the Hall unseen and made her way to the south garden which had a great arbor—heavy with white tea roses—that opened onto the moors. The breeze from the coming storm tugged at her hat, but she'd secured it safely and only reveled in the fierce gusts that swirled around her. Their fury matched her mood.

Padgett waited with her mount and young Will at his side, holding the reins of his own steed.

"My lady, it's lookin' like a frightful storm is comin'. Best ye wait until the morrow to be ridin'." The old man's gaze was riveted on the clouds looming in the distance.

She took the reins from the groom. "Don't worry, Paddy. I won't be long and I shall have young Will here to protect me."

The boy smiled and puffed out his chest. "That I will, my lady."

Padgett snorted. "I got broken sticks in the tack room what's more use than that lad. He's here to abide by Lord Denham's orders for ye not to ride alone. He ain't some knight what can rescue ye from dragons—nor storms."

Rose gazed off into the distance as if she were seeing some mythical vision. "I could use a knight at present . . . but Will shall suffice for this ride." With a sigh, she lifted her foot and Padgett, despite his worries, cupped his hands and boosted her onto the sidesaddle. "We shan't be long. I have some difficulties to ponder and riding clears my mind."

She turned the horse and the nudge of her heel put the mare into a gallop. She rode hard at the gate. Without waiting for Will, she pressed the mare toward the obstacle in her path. Vesta double-stepped in brief hesitation, then launched herself forward. The mare tucked her feet and sailed neatly over, stumbling slightly when she landed on the far side. In a flash the horse righted herself and stretched her legs out in long sure strides as her rider urged her.

Padgett watched horse and rider, and a worried frown settled on his face. Lady Rosamund was a good horsewoman, but a bad storm on the moors was nothing to ignore. Beside him, Will scrambled to climb on the small chestnut gelding.

"Bring her back afore it rains, lad."

"Aye, Paddy."

The young groom kicked his horse into a canter, but he was forced to stop and open the gate. He'd never jumped a horse in his short tenure as groom and wasn't game to start now. Lady Rose disappeared from sight before the lad was out of the enclosure.

Padgett shook his head as he watched the boy disappear over a hill after his mistress. He suspected Will would never find her once she reached Archer's Rock. But the young lady was no fool, she would rejoin the lad before riding back into the stable yard, which was all that mattered for all their sakes. He just hoped she came back before the rain. The moors could be a dangerous place during a storm.

Garth glanced up and down the upstairs hallway. He was alone at last. All the hall servants were in the kitchen preparing supper, Cherrington's valet was in the gentleman's room preparing the gentleman's wardrobe for the evening. Denham and the other gentlemen were in the billiards room. Lady Rose remained in seclusion in her chamber, likely preparing herself for her meeting with Cherrington. Thoughts of the young lady stayed his hand as he reached for the door lever. There could be little doubt that whatever she planned to say, it would not be a simpering yes. Whatever happened in the drawing room, Garth was prepared to reveal himself, if he must, to save Lady Rose from further harm.

Until then, he could pursue his true purpose for being at Denham Hall. He gripped the brass handle and pushed open the door. He stepped into Lord Wingate's bedroom, closing the door softly behind him. It was a masculine room with amber damask hangings, which complemented the oak wainscoted walls. Yet the lovely room was totally in chaos. There were numerous shirts, a colorful array of coats, and crumpled cravats tossed about at will. The young lord certainly needed a valet, but no doubt his funds were as lacking as his father's or he wouldn't have taken the chalice.

With little time to spare, Garth crossed the room to the man's wardrobe and quickly began to rifle the tall cabinet. There was nothing of interest and he moved on to the chest of drawers. He was halfway through the rosewood cabinet when the door to the room opened.

Garth looked to see Robert, Lord Wingate, frozen on the threshold.

"What are you doing in my room, Sterling?" Suspicion was written on the young man's face.

Garth moved to the bed and grabbed one of the

crumpled cravats, folding it into a neat square. "Thomas was too busy to come and ready your room for this evening, my lord. I hope you don't mind, but I thought I would help the lad by doing the chore. We are a bit at sixes and sevens with Lord Cherrington here and the staff so depleted."

The young man arched one golden brow as he watched the new butler organize his clothes before he carried them to the drawers, but Wingate's expression remained doubtful. "Well, you might have told me, I don't like my things handled by strangers."

"As you wish, my lord." Garth put down the cravat he'd been folding and started towards the door.

"Oh, you are here already. You might as well finish," Wingate grudgingly said.

Garth returned to finish the task. "Very good, my lord."

The young lord strolled over to his dressing table and picked up a silver-handled brush. He began to fuss with his golden curls but his gaze kept returning to the new butler. His face puckered into a frown as he watched the man his father had hired. He took note of the broad shoulders which required no padding and the slender waist which would be the envy of most of London's fashionable young swells. Like Rose, he didn't think the man looked like a butler.

He put down his brush, "Sterling, what are you doing working in the wilds of Yorkshire and for the pittance my father is offering? You could earn twice what you make here in London."

Garth never ceased his folding. The life history he'd concocted for Sterling, the butler, rolled off his tongue with ease. "My family is nearby, my lord. While the money is not completely what I might wish, I am near enough home to visit should the need arise." He hoped that Jack had arrived and employed some old woman to play the part of his mother, in case proof of such a family was needed for the marquess or his son. That reminded him that he'd not heard from his brother. Had something gone wrong? Or had his little brother become distracted by something or someone? It wouldn't be the first time Jack had been distracted from his duties but surely this was too important for that to happen.

Robert snorted. "As if my father would allow you to leave the Hall on personal matters if it weren't convenient for him! His comfort is primary to him. Why, I was forced to stay up playing piquet with Cherrington until the wee hours last night because my father keeps country hours and retreated to his room early." He moved to his wardrobe and began to search for something in the bottom. His muffled voice could still be heard as he continued his quest. "But not tonight. I am leaving before we dine to visit the local tavern and have some livelier entertainment." At last he pulled out a small wooden box which he took to the bed where Garth stood placing the young man's discarded coats on hangers.

Wingate dumped the contents of the box on the counterpane, then began to dig through what looked like a collection of childhood keepsakes— several shiny pebbles, a broken magnifying glass, numerous buttons, two black marbles, several stones with fossilized imprints of shells, and, to his lordship's delight, a number of guineas. As he plucked the coins from the clutter, he looked up to see the butler watching him with a questioning look in his eyes.

A bright blush rose from his pointed collar to the top of his head. "The lads at The Golden Fleece are an unenlightened lot. They won't take my vowels like gentlemen and I have been unable to go to York to my bank since I arrived."

Or to sell any of the jewels from the chalice, for which Garth was grateful, but puzzled nonetheless. Wingate had possessed the chalice for over a week. Why had he not sold a single stone? Noting the young lord's gaze on him, Garth merely vouched, "The trials of country living. Is there anything else I can do for you before I go, my lord?"

"Send Dixon to me."

"Very good, my lord." Garth exited the room, frustrated that he hadn't been able to search even a third of the possible hiding places. But if Wingate were going to be out this evening, Garth might get a second chance. That is if he still had his position after Lady Rose's stand.

Rose galloped full tilt over the moors. She rode so hard and so fast she didn't even hear the shouted greetings from her father's few tenants who were bringing home their flocks as she passed. There was no destination in her thoughts, only a desire to feel the wind on her cheeks and the powerful movement of the horse beneath her.

Like most Arabians, Vesta reveled in being allowed her head. Bred for endurance, she rarely got the opportunity to run at her top potential since she was not a racer. The animal followed the usual paths through the moors, being given little direction other than to press onward.

The sky grew darker, but Rose paid little heed, her thoughts still lodged on the horror of being forced to marry Lord Cherrington. She had promised Benny to give the matter due thought, but the very notion that the fawning dotard would be her lord and master sent shivers of fear down her spine. She'd grown up around a breeding stable much of her life and knew something of what a wife would be expected to allow. Another shiver passed over her at the thought of such intimacy with the earl. There was a brutish quality in the man despite his fashionable attire and he seemed to stare at her like she were prey and he would devour her. But what other choice did she have?

On a distant hill, Archer's Rock stood silhouetted against the storm clouds. She reined Vesta in that direction, wishing to see the town of York in the distance. Might she go there and find employment? The only true skill she possessed was the art of cookery learned at Miss Parson's.

A mirthless grin tipped her mouth since it was not something the headmistress listed as one of the accomplishments for a young lady. Parson simply used kitchen duty as punishment and Lady Rose had received her fair share of that her first year at the academy.

Yet Rose did not think anyone would employ a female as young as she for such an important task, even if she changed her name and appearance. Besides, her skills weren't sufficient to the task. Sarah and Ella had far exceeded her in the culinary arts, liking the homey quality of Cook's kitchen—and it kept them from the boring copy work that constituted lessons.

Sarah and Ella! In her misery she'd quite forgotten about them. Might she go to one of them? Ella was to live with her aunt down in Surrey which was out of the question, for Rose had no money for such a lengthy journey, but Sarah had returned to her stepmother in Shropshire which was not so great a distance. Perhaps, Rose thought, the dowager, Lady Whiting might allow her stepdaughter to have a friend visit for a month or so—until Rose could determine what she might do to support herself.

So involved in her thoughts, Rose's attention was not on her riding. As Vesta approached Archer's Rock, a young farm lad on his way home from market stepped from behind the great stone monolith into the animal's path, spooking the mare, who scuttled abruptly sideways to a halt. Unprepared, Rose hurtled out of her sidesaddle and straight into the side of the great stone which the Romans had named centuries earlier when it had been an archer's overlook for the moors. A sea of blackness consumed Rose as her head struck the edge of the granite surface.

The lad hurried to the injured female, and determined she was unconscious but without any broken bones. While he didn't recognize Lady Rosamund, he knew Lord Denham's horse in an instant. He suspected this was the lovely young daughter who he'd heard had just returned from school. He quaked in his boots that he'd been responsible for the young lady's injury, for Denham's temperament was volatile. After a moment's hesitation, the lad made a mad dash home to inform his father of the mishap. With a great deal of trepidation, the old man sent his other son to Denham Hall to summon help from the grooms to take her home, while he accompanied his eldest back to Archer's Rock. He prayed that the marquess would be understanding.

Garth made his way to the kitchens. He found Thomas almost finished with polishing the silver and requested he summon Wingate's groom as his lordship had requested.

Thomas's brows shot up. "Lord Denham don't like the grooms in the manor, Mr. Sterling. He's afraid they might get sticky fingers." The lad lifted one of the silver candelabras he'd just finished polishing.

Garth thought the marquess aught to be more concerned about his own son's thievery. "Then Wingate can explain the man's presence to his father should the need arise."

Cook, putting the lid back on the soup she'd just stirred, said, "Well, his lordship don't need to worry about young Dixon. That boy would take a musket ball for Master Robert, that devoted is he for having been rescued from his life in London. Ye can't buy loyalty like that."

Wingate rescuing street urchins! That surprised Garth. It seemed a bit out of character for a gamester. But perhaps he'd taken the chalice in a moment of desperation and was not by nature dishonest. That would definitely be to Garth's advantage, however, since he suspected that Wingate wouldn't know what exactly to do with the stones should he pry them out of the chalice.

Everyone in the kitchen started when the rear door burst open at that moment. What appeared to be an army of rain-drenched farm lads and grooms stood huddled at the arched doorway, the storm raging behind them. Cook threw her hands up and shrieked. The scullery maid, Nell, disappeared behind the door in fright. Thomas exchanged a puzzled look with Sterling.

Garth barked, "What is happening?"

A shout, "There's been an accident; send for the doctor," came from one of the group.

The burly young men edged through the doorway and there on a small gate lay Lady Rose, unconscious and drenched, a new trickle of blood oozing from a wound at the edge of her forehead. She was so deadly pale that for a moment Garth thought her dead.

Anguish seared Garth's heart. He struggled to master his emotions, even as he noted the mud on her riding habit. When had she slipped out of her room to this disaster? And had it truly been an accident? Why had he not been more vigilant? He'd heard her desperate words, yet she'd convinced him otherwise and he'd been more concerned about his own family's bit of silver and stones.

"D-does she still live?" he asked, his throat so dry the words seemed to stick.

"Aye, she does," an older groomed said, relief written on his craggy face, "but I fear it might be serious."

Garth snapped, "You," he pointed at a red-haired lad in the back, "go for the doctor at once. Thomas, find Mrs. Benson and have Lady Rosamund's room readied. Meg, the doctor will need clean linens, Cook, plenty of hot water."

Those with assignments disappeared in a rush. Garth signaled to the lads who still held the gate. "Follow me."

He led them upstairs heedless of their muddy boots to Lady Rose's room where Nurse waited, tears spilling down her lined cheeks. Garth supervised them and at last the young lady was settled on her bed.

After he dismissed the lads, he turned to Benson who stood hovering over her former charge, still weeping. "Is there anything to be done before the doctor arrives?"

She looked up at him, her face ravaged by guilt.

"It's all my fault, Sterling. I urged her to ride and even though she was upset with her father. She did not wish this marriage and, and . . ."

He moved to stand beside the old woman, patting her shoulder. "Don't blame yourself, Benson. Riding accidents happen everyday. It is a dangerous sport." He wasn't completely sure it had been an accident, but he wouldn't voice his fears to the girl's old nurse.

"But . . ."

He took the old woman's arm and turned her to face him. "We must think what should be done, not place blame." He looked at Lady Rose's pale face and worry gripped him anew. Would she survive?

Benson gathered her wits, found her handkerchief, and dried her eyes. She bustled to a nearby cabinet. "I shall remove her muddy riding habit and boots." She glanced back over her shoulder. "Has anyone told her father of the accident?"

Garth drew his gaze from the girl's lovely face. "I shall inform him at once." He strode to the door, and stopped to take one last look at the young lady in the great bed. He closed his eyes for a moment and prayed that she would survive.

In the hall, he paused. Suddenly the Chalice of Naples didn't seem so important. He hardly knew Lady Rosamund Dennison, but he promised himself that if she survived her terrible fall, he would do all in his power to save her from the Earl of Cherrington. Even if it meant never finding his family's treasure. He knew his father would be devastated, but what else could he do? The little minx might wind up killing herself if someone didn't look after her.

He headed down the hall to inform Lord Denham his daughter was gravely injured.

Four

A pall settled over Denham Hall after Doctor Mc-Cullough announced that Lady Rose's injury was indeed serious. While the young lady had suffered no broken bones, she'd sustained an injury to her brain and, in the learned Scotsman's opinion, an injury from which she might never awaken. Cook and Meg wept while Thomas went to inform the grooms. Despite the young lady's headstrong nature, she alone of the Dennison family was admired by servants and tenants alike. It was she who'd taken over her mother's duties after that lady had fallen ill. She had visited the sick, worried about the servants wages, the tenants' living conditions, and encouraged all not to leave when her father was in one of his moods.

To Garth's way of thinking, only Lord Denham and his son seemed unaffected by the accident. While Lord Wingate had dutifully inquired of his sister's health that evening at dinner, he'd seemed distracted. His father had called him to attention on more than one occasion during the meal. The marquess made only one comment that first night after everyone else had retired and he visited his daughter's room.

"Damnation, that girl will ruin everything."

Benson's face flushed red and she drove the man from the room. "If she is to recover, my lord, you must leave. I shall nurse her back to health."

Outside the sickroom, his lordship glared at Garth. "I am to be informed at once when she awakens."

"As you wish, my lord." But Garth knew he would only tell the gentleman about the young lady's condition if Nurse gave her approval. Lady Rose didn't need her father pestering her about wedding Cherrington before she regained her strength—if they were lucky enough to have her awaken.

One worry had been put to rest for Garth, when he'd learned it had been a simple riding accident and not what he'd feared, an attempt to do herself harm. Luckily for the farmer's son, Lord Denham was more concerned with keeping Cherrington from bolting than exacting his revenge on the lad or his father.

Over the course of the next few days, the doctor visited daily but each time his pronouncement remained the same. Nothing would be known about the young lady's condition unless she awoke.

Garth went about his normal routine but he often found time to stop in the sick room to take Benson a tea tray or to urge her to allow Meg a turn with Lady Rose and to rest. But the old woman was adamant, only she would sit by her dear girl. The rigors of such a task soon began to take its toll on the old nurse. Very often late at night, he would find her asleep in a chair beside the patient's bed. During those times, Garth stood over Rose and tried to will her awake but there was no improvement in her condition.

Three days passed and still there was no change in the girl's condition. Frustrated during one of his late night visits, Garth leaned over and kissed her forehead, whispering, "Come back to us, Lady Rose. I will protect you from your father." He straightened when Nurse stirred in her chair. He shouldn't be there, but a vulnerability about the girl drew him. He softly whispered a good night so as not to disturb Benson from her sleep and quietly departed the room.

In Rose's dark world, a voice seemed to beckon her. It was a comforting voice and she moved through the whirling mist determined to come out of the black void that engulfed her. The click of a door penetrated her hearing and she became more aware of her surroundings. Her eyes seemed to have weights, but at last they fluttered opened. Why was Nurse sleeping at her bedside? She couldn't remember coming to bed. Hadn't she been out riding on the moors? Her memory was elusive.

She attempted to sit up, but a sharp pounding in her head forced her to again close her eyes and lay still, yet that did little to relieve the pain. She pressed her fingers to her temple and found a bandage wrapped about her head. She must have had an accident, but how? Surely she hadn't been thrown from her horse. That hadn't happened since she was a child. The more she tried to remember, the more her head ached.

Weak, she dropped her hand back to her side. Her mind didn't seem to want to work properly and she floated in and out of a dream state, one moment with her friends in a meadow, sharing a picnic, the next back in her room, her head pounding.

The sound of a door opening penetrated the haze of pain, but to open her eyes required too much effort. Her father's voice came to her from nearby.

"Don't be a fool, Cherrington. See, even now her color improves. I tell you she will awaken and there can be a wedding."

Rose lay still, assaulted by pain caused by her father's words that ran deeper than the ache in her head. She was to marry the old earl. That is what had driven her to the moors to ride so recklessly. She still had no memory of the accident, but she knew her way of life as she'd known it at Denham Hall was in peril.

She dared not move a muscle for fear of alerting them she was awake. Tonight she simply was not strong enough to cope with the leering earl or her father. Instead, she listened to their plotting.

"Denham, I'll not be saddled with a simpleton for a bride. You know as well as I that she could awaken altered. Such a blow to the head could leave her mentally unfit. I don't care how beautiful and desirable a creature she may be, I'll not have the banns read on Sunday with her as she is now."

Rose held her breath waiting to hear what her father would say. The silence lengthened, then at last he grumbled. "Oh, very well, but do not rush off to London and look for another bride. I tell you we Dennisons are a hardy lot. She will be as she was once this passes. She's not one of those namby-pamby misses who faints at loud noises. The girl's got mettle and I tell you she shall be fine."

The earl harrumphed. "Well, I have business in London next week which cannot be delayed, but I shall return afterwards to see how the girl fares. If she is as was before the fall, I shall consent to the banns."

"Excellent, Cherrington. You will see that you shall have your beautiful young bride."

The earl mumbled something Rose could not hear, then strode from the room leaving the marquess to stand, brooding over her. As the silence lengthened, she grew frightened that he suspected her May Game. It took a great effort to still her breathing.

After several minutes, her father swore. "By Jove, if you ruin this for me, girl, I shall make your life a living hell. I need that settlement." A few moments later the door slammed shut.

It took Rose several minutes to realize that her father had been speaking aloud and not to her specifically. He still had no idea she was aware of her surroundings.

Hesitantly she opened her eyes. She moved her arms and legs with care and found while she was stiff and sore, there appeared to be no lasting injuries. The pain in her head began to lessen a bit and she felt certain with time she would recover. But nothing at Denham had changed despite her accident. Her father would marry her off as an invalid if he could. Once she recovered she would be forced to wed Cherrington in three weeks. If only she could remain in her safe warm bed forever. To not have to deal with . . .

A soft gasp escaped her as an astounding idea flashed in her mind. The marquess *and* Cherrington simply must not learn that she was awake. Rose's heart pounded with excitement, her pain forgotten in her elation. She must simply convince everyone she was unconscious. A soft snore beside her made her look to where Benny was deep in slumber.

Everyone, that is, except her dear old nurse. She would need Benny to bring her food, to tell her what was happening at the Hall with regard to Cherrington and most of all, to keep her from going crazy locked away from the outside world. She couldn't keep up this charade forever, but thinking beyond that exhausted her. A smile played about her mouth as she fell back into much needed sleep.

Late the following morning, Benson closed the door behind the departing Doctor McCullough. To her dismay, he'd avowed that nothing had changed with the patient. Nurse leaned her head against the cool oak panel, and prayed for her little Rosie. He'd become less optimistic with each passing day that the girl did not awaken.

"My dear Benny, do not worry so," a hoarse whisper came from across the room.

Benson twirled around and nearly shouted with joy at the sight of Lady Rose smiling weakly at her from her bed. She dashed across the room and grabbed the girl's hands.

"Dear child, you are awake!" Tears obscured Nurse's view of that beloved face, but she knew without a doubt her Rosie would be fine. "How do you feel? Oh, what am I thinking? I must hurry and stop the doctor from leaving. He will want to . . ."

Rose grasped Benny's hands not letting her go. "No, you must not let anyone know that I am awake."

"But child everyone is so worried about you, I must . . ." Nurse tried to remove her hands from Rose's surprisingly strong clutch, but the girl only held tighter.

"No, Benny, if my father knows that I am well, he will marry me off to Lord Cherrington."

The old woman frowned down at Rose. "What do you intend to do, child? Spend the rest of your life in bed feigning unconsciousness? You, who can scarcely remain indoors on a rainy day?"

Rose shook her head. "I only need to pretend until Cherrington gives up and goes away to plague some other young lady. At least that will buy me a bit more time to figure out what I can do before my father finds another suitor."

The two women's gazes locked and Rose smiled. "It is the only way, Benny. Otherwise I shall have to 'pike off to parts unknown,' as the Yorkshire Tykes would say."

Benson snorted, "As if you know anything about Yorkshire Tykes, my lady. Why if one of them ugly customers came within ten feet of you in town, Padgett would have made mice feet of him. And there is to be no more talking about 'piking off,' child. If you want to loll about in bed for the next twenty years, what have I to say about such odd conduct?"

A soft laugh welled inside of Rose. "You would have a great deal to say I am sure, as you always do."

The twinkle in Benson's eyes told Rose she had won the dear woman over.

Nurse patted the girl's hand. "Do you promise me you will stay completely abed for at least another week? I cannot think that if the doctor knew you'd awakened he would insist on a long recovery. No sneaking about in your room when you think it's safe."

Rose released the old woman's hands and relaxed back onto her pillows. "The way I feel at this moment, I shall willingly stay here another month."

Benson snorted. "That I will believe should I see it. Now what must I do to begin this farce?"

* * *

Word of Lady Rosamund's injury had quickly spread throughout the neighborhood. After several days with no news of the lady's condition, many friends of the late marchioness came to call and inquire about the young lady. The marquess was not at home, truly. Race week began in York on the fourth day after the young lady's accident. With Cherrington departed early to London, Denham was determined to race his horses in the Gold Cup. As he informed a poker-faced Sterling, "It ain't like I can do anything for the chit. She'll recover or she won't regardless. I have two of my best goers entered and, by Jove, I won't miss seeing them cross the finish line." With that he'd hied off to the racing grounds, his horses and grooms in tow.

Garth politely informed all callers that the young lady was no better and his lordship was not receiving. Most left without a fuss, but the nearest neighbor, the Duchess of Rayburn, was not so easily dismissed. She deluged him with a barrage of questions about the accident—which of York's doctors was attending the matter, what the girl's present condition was, and what Denham had done to assure proper supervision.

Garth dutifully answered her as best he could and when he thought she had finished at last, she surprised him when she lifted her jeweled lorgnette and peered at him rudely. "Where is Chalmers?"

"Retired, Your Grace." Garth stared at a point on the wall as he was being inspected like a horse at Tattersall's and clearly found wanting.

"What humbug! More likely that rum touch, Denham, fired the old fellow. Well, Sterling, you can tell the marquess for me that he must be all about in the head to be hiring a well-favored lad like you with an impressionable young female in the house. But then the man's attic has been to let for years in my opinion." The lady signaled to her footman to help her back into her carriage. Once inside she lowered the window. "I wish to be informed immediately upon the girl's waking."

"I shall inform his lordship of your wishes, Your Grace." There could be little doubt the marquess would ignore them, but Garth would do his duty.

The lady snorted. "If you have Lady Rosamund's best interest at heart, Sterling, you will make certain I am informed regardless of what Denham does."

Garth's blue gaze locked with the duchess' gray eyes. "I will, Your Grace."

She stared at him a moment, then, "You just might do, Sterling." With that the duchess thumped her cane on the roof and the carriage drew away from the Hall.

He watched the carriage rumble down the drive. Would the Duchess of Rayburn be willing to help Lady Rose defy her father? One could never tell about females, especially older ones who thought parents had the right to determine what was best for their daughters. She might see Cherrington as an excellent match.

About to close the door, Garth saw a strip of white cloth tied to the front gate. It had been cleverly done, looking as if someone had snagged a garment. It was the signal he'd been waiting to see for days. Jack was in Yorkshire and wanted a meeting. Garth closed the door and looked at the clock on the mantelpiece. It would be hours before he needed to put a lantern in the uppermost window to signal his brother that he would meet him at midnight. Still, he would go up and make certain the lantern he'd found was still hidden in the attic and ready.

He strode towards the stairs, but halted when Lady Rose's nurse came hurrying down the hallway carrying a tray laden with a cold collation, slices of bread, an assortment of cakes, as well as a pot of tea. His brows rose at the quantity of food on the tray. In fact, the old woman seemed to stagger with the load or had she merely been trying to escape his gaze.

A thought made his heart race. "Is Lady Rose awake?"

The old woman's face flushed and her gaze fell to the tray. "Of course not. Do you not think I would have shouted such joyous news from the roof top?"

His gaze returned to the food. "I only thought . . . never mind. Allow me, Benson." He stepped into her path.

Nurse appeared unhappy at the sight of him and even attempted to sidled from his reach. "That won't be necessary, Sterling. I am in a hurry."

He took the tray from her reluctant hands. "Is Meg not sitting with our patient? You should take this time to rest and enjoy your meal in the servants' hall."

The lady's face flamed red. "Why, no, I didn't need to bother Meg when I want just a bite to eat."

As Garth's gaze roved over the repast he was tempted to tell the woman this might be a bite for a lion, but for a female it would constitute a feast for a week. But he held his tongue for she'd done more than her share of taking care of the patient. If she wanted to gorge herself, who was he to criticize her, and she could certainly use a bit of fattening up. He turned and strode up the stairs. Nurse followed close on his heels protesting that she was quite capable of carrying a tray.

Without responding to her chatter, Garth continued down the hall. At Lady Rose's door, he shifted the tray into one hand and reached for the handle when Benson shrieked, "Sterling!"

Garth's brows rose as he looked at the woman who suddenly looked as if she were hunted by hounds. "What's wrong?"

In near hysteria, she said, "Oh, I thought you were about to drop the tray."

"Are you feeling quite the thing?" Garth peered at her closely. There were dark circles under her lined eyes, her cheeks were flushed and her hands were nervously fidgeting with her apron, but she appeared healthy otherwise.

The old woman gave a shrill laugh. "Only a bit tired. I shall be better once I dine."

He opened the door, wondering if the old woman had always been this strange. Without a word he took the tray into Lady Rose's room. His gaze was immediately drawn to the girl in the four-poster. After he put the tray down, his scrutiny of her intensified. Perhaps it was wishful thinking, but he thought Lady Rose looked better. The color in her cheeks, while not rosy, was no longer ghostly white, and her lovely mouth seemed less drawn. About to ask Nurse if she'd noticed any signs of her patient's recovery, Garth found his arm gripped by Benson, and she drew him to the door. "Thank you, Sterling. That will be all."

Before he knew what had happened he'd been ushered from the room, the door slammed in his face. He stood a moment wondering if age or fatigue made Nurse so strange. He would suggest that Meg again try to convince Benson to get some rest and allow her to sit up with Lady Rose.

At that moment raised voices could be heard down the hall. They came from the direction of Wingate's room, which was the last on the right. The lord was still abed, or so Garth thought. Lord Wingate had remained home from the races to sleep. He'd informed his father at dinner the night before that he wouldn't be accompanying him, since his father's entourage of grooms and horses intended to go at first light. Denham had taken exception and the argument was still in progress when Garth had withdrawn to bring the next course. The news had been disappointing. It was one more lost opportunity for him, since he'd hope to get another chance to search Wingate's room while he was out. Strange, since his night of gambling at the Golden Fleece, the gentleman had remained close to the Hall.

Garth slipped down the carpeted hallway, drawing closer as he tried to hear who was with the young gentleman. Suddenly the door to Wingate's room opened. Garth heard the young lord's voice. "I must think about this. I shall have a decision after the races."

Dixon, his lordship's groom stepped into the hallway, hat in hand. "There is no reason not to . . ." he halted what he'd been about to say on spying the butler. "G-good day, Mr. Sterling." Without completing what he'd intended to say to his master, he hurried down the hall.

Wingate appeared at the door, a scowl on his face. He was still in his shirtsleeves, his cravat hanging half tied. "What do you want?"

Garth, thinking quickly, said, "Your father ordered

us not to hold breakfast for you, my lord. I wondered if you might like a tray served in your room."

His lordship's face brightened. "I'm famished, old man, an excellent notion. I begin to think this trip to Yorkshire shall bring me luck."

Garth thought it would be pointless to remind the young man that his sister was lying gravely injured just down the hall. "I shall only be a moment, my lord."

He returned downstairs to find the kitchen in crisis. Thomas was nowhere to be found and the kitchen fireplace was smoking, Meg and the scullery maid, Nell, were exchanging words over which one Dixon had winked at before leaving, and Cook was in the boughs over the small size of the turkey the Home Farm had sent, declaring she'd seen wrens with more meat on their bones.

By the time the new butler got everything sorted out below stairs and the promised tray to Lord Wingate, the marquess and a retinue of racing friends had arrived. There was a great celebration, for his lordship's horse had won in the first race of the day. Garth's day was much engaged in his duties and it was well after nine that evening before he was able to slip away and put the lantern in the window to signal his brother that he'd received his sign and would be at the gate that night.

Nourishment did much to improve Rose's strength. The cold collation brought by the butler had revived her energy. Fortuitously, Benson managed to smuggle a warm meal from the kitchen for Rose's supper. A light headache persisted but she didn't tell her old nurse of the nagging pain, fearful the old woman would worry. Every time Rose suggested she wanted to rise Benson would fret anew.

Benson still hadn't recovered her wits after the fright Sterling had given her that morning. She was quite convinced their little ruse would never work. She lamented that in the end very likely it would be she who would be tossed into the cold world while Rose would be married to the dreadful old earl.

It was well after eleven that evening and Rose wanted to sit beside her bedroom window for a bit of fresh air. She was convinced that would do much to revive her and put an end to the nagging pain.

"You shall be the death of me yet, child." The old woman sat rocking beside the young lady's bed. "You should be sleeping, not gaping out the window. Just remember, we might not be so lucky next time. I might not be here to shout a warning."

"I tell you, Benny, I was not out of bed. I am not such a henwit to be up during the daylight hours." She rubbed a finger along the edge of the bandage where the pain concentrated. "Besides, I heard you, long before you began shrieking the man's name at the door. All I had to do was to close my eyes and lay still. Don't worry so. I shall be very careful. I know to lock my door would create suspicion. But at night there is no reason I cannot sit up. Why, we haven't heard a bit of stirring downstairs since after ten."

Benson crossed her arms over her chest. "It is too soon for you to be up. Close those eyes and go to sleep."

Rose sighed and did as she was bid. Still sleep did not come. But then how could it when she'd been sleeping for days? Did being unconscious constitute sleep? Well, Rose didn't think so, but she had slept the entire afternoon while Benny had watched over her. Tonight she was too unsettled to sleep. The good news was that Cherrington had left for Town, but the bad news was the man intended to return in a few days and see how his prospective bride was doing. She might have to continue the charade for weeks, nay even months, but she was willing to do anything to avoid marriage to the earl.

A soft snore beside Rose alerted her that Nurse was asleep. Restless, she decided that she must move about a little or she would never get to sleep again. She slowly tossed back the covers and lowered her feet as she sat up. There was a strange spinning of the room and she closed her eyes, taking deep breaths. After a moment the sensation went away. She opened her eyes and the room had righted itself. Perhaps she shouldn't get up. Benny kept saying she must be careful.

A breeze billowed out the curtains where Benny had opened the window and the temptation became too much. Rose slid off the bed and stood for a moment to get the feeling in her legs back. As a precaution she leaned over and blew out the candle, fearing she might be seen if someone were about, then she crossed to the window. Her knees seemed a bit shaky, but otherwise she experienced no difficulty. She pushed the mullioned panel outward and reveled in the nighttime breeze. The landscape was awash in moonlight and the moors looked beautiful yet lonely. Was this the way she would spend the rest of her life? Hiding from the world, being alone, and living in cold and darkness? She'd never been one to fear the night. She had her mother to thank for that. Often they would walk in the garden well after dark, talking of all Lady Denham's hopes for her daughter. But even then Rose had known they were mere

dreams. Her father had managed to run through the
fortune her mother brought to the marriage long
before Rose was out of leading strings.

A muffled noise in the distance distracted Rose
from her melancholy thoughts. She peered into the
garden below and suddenly caught sight of someone
hurrying across the lawn. Was Robert slipping out at
night? But as she watched the figure move swiftly
away from where she stood she realized it couldn't
be her brother. He'd come home around ten, deep
in his cups, and Thomas and Sterling had helped
him to his room. Rose realized her brother would
scarcely be able to get out of bed in the morning,
much less again this evening.

The figure stopped at the garden gate, then
turned and looked back at the house. Rose, afraid
her white nightcap and gown with her gold curls
dangling loose might be visible in the moonlight,
drew back from the window. But in that instant she
caught another glimpse of the tall figure with the
broad shoulders. Thomas was too short and her father too heavy for the silhouetted figure and the only
other man in the house was Sterling. What was the
butler doing out this late at night? She waited a moment, then peeked out the window but there was no
one there. He must have gone through the gate.

Whatever was Sterling up to? Was he having a
tryst? The idea left Rose feeling quite uncomfortable
and she didn't know why. It was none of her concern
if Sterling were meeting one of the maids in the
shrubbery. She knew those kinds of things happened, but still she found herself disappointed that
he would involve himself in such amoral activities.

Suddenly the night air no longer invigorated her.
She felt strangely queasy and on the verge of tears.

She made her way back to her bed and crawled under the covers. Sterling could meet as many maids as he liked. She had her own problems to contend with and no telling how many more of these lonely nights ahead. With a sigh she turned on her side, but slumber escaped her. The sun was coming up before Rose finally fell asleep.

Five

"What took you so long?" Jack Fenton stepped from behind a tall oak which bordered the estate wall as his brother strode through the gates of Denham. His appearance would have startled his friends of the Ton. Gone were the fashionable clothes and Hessians. Instead he'd adopted the attire of the Yorkshire farmers, dressed in a wheat colored frock coat over a long brown waistcoat with tan breeches, brown stockings, and muddy brogans. He clutched a large floppy hat in his hand as he came forward.

"A butler's duties are never done. And might I ask you the same question?" Garth clapped his brother on the shoulder in the moonlit darkness and moved to stand in the shadows of the oak. He thought he'd seen someone standing at a window, but when he'd looked again the figure was gone. It would never do to have to explain what he was doing out at night.

"Mother had the vapors when she saw me in this rig and begged me not to go. She's convinced one of us is likely to end up with a musket ball in us or worse, dead. It took nearly a day for Father to calm her fears enough to allow me to slip away. After that it's been mostly rainy weather and flooded roads. But I've got what you wanted." He dug into his pocket and pulled out a sheet of paper. "I had to go north to find the woman, since too many people in York knew the marquess. She lives in a cottage outside Thirk about a mile off the Great North Road. You veer to your left after the Roman ruins. I've described you to her and she's fully prepared to vow you are her loyal son, a hard working butler, should someone come to ask."

Garth took the paper and slipped it into coat. "Excellent, but there is so much happening at Denham, no one is questioning my appearance." Only Lady Rose had pressed him about Chalmers's disappearance and until she recovered, she offered no danger to him.

"Then you've had no luck finding the chalice." Jack's voice was full of disappointment.

"Wingate arrived with his sister only a few days ago and there's been a *guest,*" Garth's tone grew cold at the word, then after a moment he continued, "I've only been able to partially search your friend's room. Now with Lady Rosamund's accident, the house has had a steady stream of callers. I don't know when I'll be able to get inside his chambers again to search, but I'm almost certain he hasn't sold any of the jewels."

"I heard of the accident. Even the farmers at the local tavern are speaking about her. Lady Rose seems quite a favorite with the people. Is she as lovely as they say?"

Garth turned and gazed back at the Hall as the vision of the young lady at the door that first morning rose in his mind. "She would be a Diamond of the First Water in London."

"Is the accident as bad as they are saying?"

A strange knot tightened in Garth's stomach. "She's been unconscious for nearly four days. She just lies in that great bed so still and quiet it tears at one's insides since she is so young and innocent."

Jack couldn't see the nuances of his brother's expression in the darkness, but his tone betrayed him. Somehow a chit of a girl had managed to get under his brother's skin, which surprised Jack. He had assumed that his brother would never fall in love, that Garth would make one of those ghastly arranged marriages where the female had a fortune and title but little else to interest a man. It wasn't that his brother disliked women, only that estate matters seemed to dominate his thoughts, and he did not notice women's sidelong glances and obvious ploys to attract his attention.

The younger Fenton laid a hand on Garth's shoulder. "Don't give up hope. She might yet be all right."

Garth stiffened at his brother's tone. "You misunderstand. It is not that I am involved with the lady, merely concerned for her safe recovery. But we have other matters to worry us. Have you any attire other than that rough rig?"

Jack looked down at his disguise. "Of course. Once we get the chalice back I shall once again become the dashing gentleman that I am." He swirled his hand in front of him, reminiscent of cavaliers in days of yore.

"Don't you mean 'fop'?" Garth couldn't resist the jibe.

"Fop," Jack sputtered, between clenched teeth. Then he heard his brother's chuckle and his pique faded. "I know you care nothing for Society and fashion, but . . . well, I like London."

"We each are entitled to our likes and dislikes, Jack. I am not criticizing you, only roasting you. But for the present, I want you to like York. Search out all the pawn and jewelry shops in the town. Inquire about anyone selling loose stones. Say you are hoping to purchase rubies or emeralds of a certain size. If Wingate is trying to sell them, we want to recover them as quickly as possible."

Jack nodded his head. "Anything else?"

"Don't attract attention and whatever you do don't stumble across Wingate at one of the better inns or gaming houses. He might take the chalice and run if he suspects you are looking for it. If you need to see me, leave a message at the Brown Pigeon at the crossroads. My footman is a man who likes a tankard most nights and he can't read so there's no danger there." The sound of a lone set of hoofbeats approaching on the road set him on alert. "We'd better go before I am discovered. If I should by chance recover the chalice, where might I find you?"

"I'm at the Blue Boar Inn on Castlegate. You needn't worry about Wingate darkening the door there. The sheets are damp and the grog is watered." Jack paused a moment and his youthful exuberance could not be contained. "They say the famous highwayman, Dick Turpin, stayed there before he was hanged. They even displayed his body in the public rooms for several days."

"Let us hope the clientele is improved since then." Garth's gaze was riveted in the direction of the unknown rider.

"Well, there's a doxy they call Queen Mab, who tells me they haven't hanged any of the patrons in the last thirty years or so, but the beadle makes regular visits to haul off some of the local poachers on occasion." There was laughter in his voice.

"Be careful, Jack. This is no game," Garth urged his sibling.

In a more sober tone, the lad replied, "I shall."

Garth clasped his brother's shoulders then disappeared back inside the gates of Denham. Jack waited until the rider passed, heading towards York, then went to his own horse and followed the man at a distance toward town. He thought it a shame that his brother seemed drawn to Denham's daughter. But Garth had always been the sensible one. He would never tie the Fentons to a family like Wingate's no matter how enchanting this Lady Rosamund might be.

The hardest part of pretending to be unconscious was the daily visits of Doctor McCullough. He would poke and prod, open Lady Rose's eyes and listen to her heartbeat. The young lady was forced to lie still, slow her breathing, and respond to none of the rough handling. She would listen to his concerned voice asking Benson about the patient during the previous day. Had she taken any gruel? Was there any sign that she was responding to noise or voices? Had she spoken, even to mumble a few words in her sleep?

Things were equally hard for Nurse, forced to deceive, well aware of what was at stake. She swore there had been no improvement in the girl.

At the end of the first week, the doctor finished his examination of his patient, then sadly shook his head. "I fear the young lady might never awaken, Nurse. The damage appears more severe than I had surmised. It is quite a strange thing. All the signs indicate she should be waking, yet you have seen no stirring." He tugged the spectacles from his nose.

Rose heard the eagerness in the old woman's

voice. "Not a bit of it, Doctor. Perhaps it's best to leave the child alone and what will be will be." Benson dreaded each new visit of the doctor. Few others in the household pressed her so for details, with the exception of Sterling. He always managed to search her out when she was below stairs to inquire about the girl.

McCullough grunted as he closed his bag. "Leave her alone? You refer to his lordship from what I hear."

Lord Denham stopped by several times each day to ask if the girl was awake. Yet no one attributed his excessive attention as concern for his daughter, only his selfish need to use her to barter for the estate.

As if mentioning the marquess had proven a bad omen, the door to Lady Rose's room opened and in strode Lord Denham. He peered down at his daughter as one would a science specimen, without any great attachment. "Have you any news, McCullough?"

"I fear none that you will wish to hear, my lord." The doctor picked up his bag and edged back towards the door. "There is little else I can do, my lord. The brain is mysterious in the way it works, and I fear that whatever has happened inside Lady Rose's head is beyond my meager skills. Benson is doing everything the girl needs, but I fear that your daughter might never awaken."

Denham's mouth grew grim. "Then begone man, and stop wasting my time and money! Don't return if you cannot heal her." His lordship never looked up as the door shut behind the departing physician. Appearing to forget that Benson was there, he grumbled, "Females are more trouble than they are worth. What the devil am I to tell Cherrington when he returns?" He then marched out of the room without so much as a backward glance at his daughter.

From that day hence, things became easier for the two women. There were few visitors to the lady's bed-chamber and therefore few chances that their charade might be uncovered. It was as if the members of the household quite forgot that Lady Rose existed, or they were so overworked they had no time to spare to visit her room. Still, each time they would see Benson slip into the kitchen for a tray of food or to wash one of her ladyship's night rails they would ask about the patient and Nurse would sadly shake her head. Only Sterling continued to visit the young lady, but even Benson noted that he seemed a bit distracted and rarely stayed above a moment.

The races continued in York and several gentle-men interested in buying from a winning stable came to stay with the marquess and inspect his current crop of frisky yearlings. Robert, too, found London friends had come north for the Gold Cup and he invited Sir Marcus Ripley to stay at Denham, which kept the meager staff of the Hall busy. Lord Denham spared little thought for his daughter except when the Earl of Cherrington's name was mentioned, then he grew morose and drank heavily before being helped to bed by Sterling.

As to Rose, her health rapidly improved with her forced seclusion. The headaches disappeared and the wound near her scalp began to heal. In the day-time, she stayed abed with the curtains drawn. Surprisingly she slept soundly most days, but late at night when the house grew quiet, after Benson pulled out the trundle and retired, Rose's day would begin. In only her night rail and dressing gown, she would play solitary card games, sketch pictures, write letters to Sarah and Ella which she put aside to post later, feast on the tray of food Benson smuggled from the larder during the day, then read until the sun lit the morning sky.

Unfortunately, her old nurse couldn't spend the entire night awake with her. They knew it would attract unwanted attention, unless her servant made an appearance below stairs at least several times during the day, so the older woman slumbered on the trundle, leaving Rose to amuse herself alone.

The only problem her nighttime life created had been the vast number of candles that were burned to brighten what she called her prison. They had tried the tallow candles used in the kitchens, but the heavy odor seemed to permeate not only the room, but into the hallway as well. The pungent fumes even made Rose cough. Fearful that her father or brother might smell the distinctive tallow stench and come to inspect, the women determined that only the good candles could be used. Somehow, Rose didn't ask how, Benson managed to keep the room suitably lit for her young charge with the household's more expensive wax tapers.

The pair never discussed how long they could continue this charade. It was clearly understood that until Cherrington returned and determined that Lady Rose was beyond his reach things would stay as they were.

Despite her best intentions, Rose soon grew bored, confined as she was to that single room. Benson did her best to bring the neighborhood gossip she heard in the kitchens and a variety of books from the library. She even stayed up unusually late to play backgammon or cards with Rose, but still the girl became progressively more restless. By the fifth lonely night awake, she began to pace soon after Benson fell asleep. The room, despite its large dimension and fine furnishings, began to feel as if it were pressing in on Rose's restive spirit.

Danger of discovery lay outside her door, especially with guests in the house, but Rose soon became convinced that madness would overtake her if she stayed here one moment longer. She stepped to the door and put her hand on the lever, then she recovered her wits. She moved back to the small circle of light and grabbed a deck of cards. She could not risk going outside and forced herself to begin a game of Patience—the fifth one that night. She'd barely laid out the proper pattern for the game, when she dropped the remaining deck and leaned back in the chair knowing that she wanted to weep in frustration. What good was this doing? Even if Cherrington gave up his suit, her father would find another wealthy gentleman to sell her to once she reappeared outside these walls. She couldn't spend the rest of her life in her bedchamber.

With a disheartened glance at the clock she realized it was only midnight. How would she survive another long night alone? She pushed out of the chair and moved to the window where she drew the curtain aside. A full moon hovered just above the horizon, bathing the landscape in it full brightness. It was as if some enchantment hung over the moors that seemed to beckon her against her will. What harm could there be to go out? Her father, brother, and all the servants were asleep. No one would know.

Tamping down the voice that urged her not to be foolish, Rose hurried to the wardrobe and pulled out her riding habit. In minutes she was dressed and she slipped from the room, but not before she whispered, "Forgive me, Benny. I know what you would say, but I must go."

* * *

The longcase clock at the head of the stairs had chimed midnight nearly thirty minutes before, yet Garth was still not finished with his duties. He'd sent Thomas and Meg to bed, knowing they would need to be up early for Lord Denham's guests who intended going to Kavesmire Racing Grounds early.

Garth walked to the wall-mounted candle brace and snuffed out two of the flames when he realized that two of the candles were missing from the gilt brace which held ten. As he looked at the matching brace on the opposite side of the mirror, he realized that two were missing from that one as well. This was not the first time he'd discovered missing candles in the main rooms. Who might be using so many candles? Wax candles were expensive and they were kept locked in the silver closet to which only he had the key. He would have to speak with Thomas in the morning and determine if one of the servants was stealing them. At this rate he would have to apply to Lord Denham to increase the house accounts or sit in the dark.

Garth finished snuffing the candles on the west wall then moved to the opposite side of the great hall to put out the candles there. As he approached the wall he noted a pair of black lacquered cabinets with marble tops on short cabriole legs set into a small recess in the wall. It would be the perfect place to store something the size of the chalice, if one stepped into the great hall and needed to be rid of an illicit item before he was seen. With a glance over his shoulder, Garth moved to stoop in front of the cabinet. There was a key in the lock, which he turned and the door swung open. The cabinet proved deeper than it looked and he began to rummage around in its shadowy depth, hoping beyond hope that Wingate might have hidden the chalice there.

The muted sound of rapidly moving footsteps on the carpeted stairs caused Garth to start. He had been certain everyone was abed, or so he thought. He turn round, pushing the doors shut, trying to school his features to his usual passive expression, but that was impossible when he spied the owner of the footsteps.

Coming down the stairs at a near run was Lady Rosamund Dennison. The lady looked as healthy as last he'd seen her days earlier, save a small red scar at the edge of her golden curls which lay loose and unruly about her shoulders. Stranger still, the lady was dressed in her green riding habit.

The soft bang of the cabinet doors closing behind him echoed in the hall, causing the lady to freeze at the foot of the stairs. Their eyes locked.

"Sterling!"

"Lady Rose!"

Garth's mind was in turmoil. How could she be here and appearing as if nothing had happened? He'd worried about her health and yet she appeared not the least out of curl as his gaze swept over her. At last he found his tongue. "Should I wake the family and inform all that you are awake at last?" Then he arched one brow as another thought occurred, "Or has this all been a hoax, my lady?"

"No! No!" She took several steps towards him, fear transformed her face, making her lovely mouth tremble. "Pray do not tell anyone you have seen me, especially not Father. I *was* truly injured, then"—she looked at her gloved hands—"well, it does no harm to anyone to pretend to be incapacitated for a while longer. I—I cannot marry that dreadful man." She lifted her head, her beautiful green eyes full of entreaty. "Will you keep my secret?"

Garth caught his breath. One couldn't deny such a heartfelt appeal. Besides, he had too many secrets of his own to be revealing hers. "I will, Lady Rose."

"Will you give me your word?"

"I promise." It was madness to be involving himself in this young lady's machinations against her father, to risk his position, but Garth didn't have it in him to stand idly by while the marquess forced her into the kind of bondage a marriage to Cherrington would be.

Relief flooded her features and Lady Rose tugged a smile from the depth of her unhappiness. Something intense flared inside Garth as she looked up at him. It was a sensation which he didn't recognize and at last he attributed it to mere lust. Her delicate beauty made him want to taste her lovely mouth, to run his hands over that soft skin—suddenly realizing where his thoughts were heading, he grabbed the brass snuffer from the marble tabletop. He turned his back on her and started to extinguish the candles that still remained. "Good night, my lady."

"Thank you, Sterling."

He heard her footsteps retreating and a deep fury built in him to be having such lascivious thoughts about a gently bred female. She certainly was no child but neither was she a woman of the world. His family's chalice was his priority. He had no business involving himself with a female whose circumstances were little different from most females her age. Only she had chosen to play some deep game with her father, unlike most dutiful daughters.

Suddenly the sound of the front door lock turning caught his attention.

"What the devil!" Garth turned to see Lady Rose about to depart the Hall. Surely she had taken leave of her senses to be going out after dark and without her maid. With long strides he closed the gap between them. He grabbed the weathered front door as she drew the portal open.

"Where do you think you are going, my lady? It is past midnight." His tone was gentle as if dealing with a naughty child.

"I intend to ride on the moors." She sounded so matter of fact, one might think it were a bright sunny day and there was nothing unusual in going out.

"You cannot, my lady."

The lady stiffened. "I can and I shall, Sterling." She tugged the door free from his grasp and stepped past him into the moonlight.

Garth followed. This was dangerous ground. His position limited his ability to demand she stay, but his principles wouldn't allow him to disregard her recklessness. "'Tis not safe for a young lady to be abroad at night. You endanger yourself as well as the horse on such uneven terrain in the dark. What if someone recognizes you and informs your father, my lady? You must not go."

Lady Rose chuckled, but she never drew her gaze from the rolling hills beyond the estate gates. "Who, Sterling?" She swept her arm in the direction of the moors. "Even the animals are in their burrows this late. There is no servant nor tenant awake and . . ." She looked at him, the light from the open doorway illuminating her lovely face, " I shall go quite mad if I do not go out. As to the danger, I know those paths like the back of my hand. Do not think this is my first time to ride at night." She stepped to the gravel path, then looked back at him. "Remember, you promised not to betray me." Her boots crunched the limestone pebbles as she moved down the path toward the stables.

Garth swore under his breath. He'd been foolish not to realize what such a promise might entail, but one thing was certain, he could not let her go alone. He tugged the front door closed and followed the lady.

Rose was halfway to the stables before she realized the butler had followed her. His black suit of clothes rendered him nearly invisible in the dark shadows as he advanced toward her, but he made no effort to hide himself, boldly striding along the path.

"What are you doing, Sterling?"

"I intend to accompany you, my lady, unless you mean to wake one of the grooms."

Annoyed, she snapped, "Of course I shan't wake anyone and you cannot go with me." Chalmers might have railed against her going, but he would never have attempted to intrude on her ride. "Go back to the Hall."

"Only when you return, Lady Rose." In the darkness he was a towering silhouette standing beside her, yet she didn't feel the least bit afraid, only annoyed that he did not follow her instructions to depart.

"I am in no danger in the remote area. I can take care of myself."

In a flash he grabbed her arms and drew her close, her face only inches from his. She could feel his warm breath as he spoke. "Lady Rose, what would you do if some villain were to get his hands on you like this?"

"I—I won't allow anyone . . ." Her heart was pounding, but fear was no part of that emotion.

"Could you stop me, my lady, if I wanted to kiss you at this very moment?" he asked in a husky voice.

"I would . . . you would never . . ." Rose found her senses in a jumble as was her mind. What would his kiss be like? Would she find pleasure? But, to her surprising disappointment, he didn't kiss her, instead he released her and stepped back.

"No woman should be out alone in the dark, my lady. I am going with you."

It took a few moments to get her thoughts ordered and remember that he hadn't wanted to kiss her, merely make a point. But he simply didn't understand. No one could gain such power over her while she was on horseback. What right did he have to try and interfere, anyway? He was her father's butler. A servant who was trying to tell her she could not do as she wanted. Anger bubbled up inside her that he'd made her feel defenseless if only for a moment. About to protest further, she realized that it didn't matter if he came along. Few people could rival her on horseback. She would simply ride off and leave her unwanted protector behind. After all, how good would a mere butler be on one of her father's highbred Arabians?

"Very well, Sterling, if you insist you may ride with me, but you must saddle your own mount."

"I think I can manage if you can, my lady."

Rose peered at him in the darkness. There had been a hint of amusement in that voice, but she could not see his features well enough to know if he were mocking her. Without further argument, she set off for the stable. Over her shoulder she said, "We must be very quiet. A groom sleeps in the hayloft. I shall point out a horse, but you must find your own tack. Once saddled, we shall have to walk the horses to the East gate, then we can mount."

The butler made no comment, merely staying at her side with annoying constancy.

A lone lantern hung from a pole in the middle aisle of the main stable, dimly lighting the long row. The pungent smell of manure, leather, and hay filled the building, giving Rose a feeling of truly being home. She had spent many of her days here with Padgett teaching her to ride; then after her mother died, she'd found solace on horseback. Her gaze skimmed along the line of horses in their stalls as she contemplated which would be the most difficult to handle for this annoying man beside her. She spied the dark eyes of Black Satin, an obstinate horse sired by the reigning champion of the Turf, Atlas. The breeding had been excessively expensive for her father and he'd had great hopes, but the compact Arabian colt had proven too high-strung to race. To Lord Denham's dismay, the animal had injured more than one jockey who had attempted to race him. Her father had been forced to put the temperamental animal out to stud, pinning his hopes on future foals sired. Relieved of the responsibility to ride the unmanageable steed, the grooms had taken to calling the horse Satan behind the marquess' back.

For a brief moment, Rose contemplated urging Sterling to take the stallion; then she realized she didn't want to kill him, just delay him enough so she could slip away. She surveyed the nearby animals and a smile tipped her mouth as she spotted a gelding in the last stall that the grooms used for errands. She pointed to the chestnut horse.

"Take Delphi. He's least likely to put you on the ground."

To her surprise, Sterling appraised the animal in one swift glance. "Do not take me for a flat, Lady Rose. I would do better to follow on foot than to mount that old hack. What about the black here?"

Rose opened her mouth to warn him about Black Satin, but angered by his impertinence she said, "Suit yourself, Sterling, but don't blame me if you end up with a broken head."

"I shall manage, my lady."

She looked into his eyes and that annoying twinkle was still there. Why did she get the feeling the man was roasting her at every turn? "If you must go with me, be at the rear of the mare's stable in ten minutes." She marched off in the direction of Vesta, hoping he would not appear on time. To her chagrin, he was there before her with a restless Satin tacked and ready to ride.

"Follow me." Rose led the way through the rear paddock until they reached a gate that opened onto the road south. To her surprise Sterling stepped forward and cupped his hands, giving her a boost up on her mare. He then mounted but Satin started to sidle away from her horse.

"Steady," he said gently. He tightened his hold on the reins and the stallion quieted, seeming to recognize a master's hand.

Rose smiled in the darkness, knowing that Sterling hadn't seen the animal at his worst as yet. She nudged Vesta into a light trot. The road stretched like a silver ribbon before them in the moonlight. Her eyes grew accustomed to the darkness and the full contour of the land was evident.

Sterling edged his horse close to her. He sat the animal very well. He was truly a puzzle, for there was little about him to suggest he was a butler. "Sterling, may I ask how you like working for my father?"

There was a moment's hesitation then he responded. "You would not expect me to answer that truthfully, would you?"

Rose laughed, surprised by his honest response. "I suppose not. I cannot think being in service a pleasant life. Being at the whim of people who often give you not the least thought."

"Especially when I considered such whims dangerous, Lady Rose."

Rose's cheeks warmed with guilt, and she pushed her horse into a canter. The sound of her companion coming up behind her spurred her to urge Vesta into a full gallop. The animal pulled away briefly, but the sound of Satin closing in, warned her that the man was sticking to her like a determined *duenna*.

The horses raced along the road churning up a cloud of dust behind. For a moment it seemed as if they were the only two people on earth as they hurtled over the Yorkshire moor and a sense of freedom washed over Rose. This is what she'd missed most during her exile at school. She glanced to her left and was startled to discover Sterling, not only managing Satin without the least difficulty, but gaining ground on her. She drove her horse harder determined to reach the crest of the hill before him.

It was perhaps a childish thing to do but she possessed a need to let him know that she didn't need him interfering in her ride. She could take care of herself on horseback. As they topped the rise of a hill a vixen and two small kits darted across their path. Vesta, in full flight, reared up, nearly unseating Rose. The sudden halt threw her forward, dislodging her hat, which flew to the road. The jarring halt gave her a momentary dizzy feeling.

Sterling sailed Black Satin over the family of wild foxes, then brought the horse to a neat halt. He trotted back to her side as she slid from her horse.

"Are you unwell, my lady?"

She rubbed at her temple which ached again. Perhaps she was not as fully recovered as she thought. She stooped to retrieve the round topped beaver with green ribbon and a spinning started in her head. "I . . . I don't know why, but I feel strange . . ." Rose didn't realize she'd begun to weave a bit until she felt strong hands pluck her from the ground. To her utter amazement, Sterling lifted her off her feet and sat her in front of him on Satin, his strong arms encircling her.

"W-what are you doing? Put me down." Her protest sounded weak even to her own ears. She could not deny that she felt safe in the man's arms.

"You should not have come, my lady. 'Tis too soon since your accident."

Rose wanted to protest again, yet the strange dizziness persisted. Despite her better judgment, she relaxed against him. "I think it was only the bumpy halt that startled me, Sterling. If you give me a few moments, I shall be able to manage to ride back unassisted."

"We are going back to the Hall at once, my lady."

Rose didn't argue as he took Vesta's reins from her hand. He turned the stallion round and walked the animals back to the rear gate. Every nerve in her body seemed to be aware of his masculine appeal. The scent of his sandalwood soap, the feeling of those strong muscular arms guiding his horse, the coarse texture of his coat against her cheek, and the sinewy strength of his legs where hers dangled. She'd never been held so close by a man and her senses were reeling. When they reached the entry, he dismounted, then lifted her down, holding her close for a moment when she swayed slightly.

A breathless sensation overwhelmed her as she felt

his hands still at her waist. She looked up into his face, but the angle shadowed his features from the moonlight and she didn't know what he was experiencing.

He huskily asked, "Will you be able to walk back to the manor unassisted?" There was just the briefest of pauses and when she didn't reply he asked, "My lady?"

Those last two words suddenly reminded her she was in the arms of a butler. She stepped back, "I—I am better, Sterling." But was she? A dawning realization had finally struck her. He might be a servant, but he was still a handsome man, which made her vulnerable to his sheer manly allure.

He opened the gate for her. "Return to the Hall and I shall put the horses back in their stalls and brush the dust from their coats."

Without a backward glance, Rose strode across the paddock and through the stable back toward the manor, her mind and body a jumble of conflicting thoughts and sensations. It wasn't until she was safely back in her room and dressed again in her night rail that she stopped to wonder how Sterling had learned to ride so well. Then she decided that the less she thought about the man the better.

Six

Benson, unaware of all that had occurred while she slept, rose early the following morning to purloin some food from the larder before Cook had the time to note what the old woman was about. Nurse, surveying the shelves, started when a shadow darkened the doorway.

"I know your secret." Garth stepped inside the pantry.

The old woman's hand jerked and she spilled a plate of macaroons at his words. "W-what do you mean, Mr. Sterling? I have no s-secrets."

After taking a look around to make certain none of the other servants were close at hand, Garth closed the door. "She didn't tell you? I feared as much."

Benson's eyes grew wider and she seemed to gasp for a breath. "Who didn't tell me what?"

"Lady Rose didn't tell you about her midnight ride on the moors?"

Nurse stooped and began to gather the coconut treats from the floor, her head bowed so she didn't have to look him in the eye. "Mr. Sterling, have you been at his lordship's brandy? Lady Rose is unconscious and has been this past week."

Garth knelt and grabbed one of the old woman's

hands. "Then was that a ghost I encountered sneaking out of the Hall in her riding habit last night? Perhaps it was a ghost I helped to mount on the little gray mare and doubtless it was a ghost I had to carry back to the stables after she was nearly tossed from her horse."

Benson's hand clutched at her heart, horror etched on her face. "She wouldn't be so foolish to ride again so soon and after dark."

"She would and she did, despite me urging her not to go. My promise not to betray her to her father left me powerless to stop her. Since you already know of her little May Game I turn to you, Mrs. Benson. Lady Rose would not listen to my warnings. But she must heed someone. Do not allow her to leave the Hall at night. There is not only the danger of her father discovering he's being duped, which was foremost in her mind, but the danger of some unscrupulous villain finding her alone on the moors, which was my great worry."

Tears welled up in Benson's eyes. "I didn't know. I fear fatigue got the better of me. I must have fallen asleep too early." She pulled a handkerchief from her cuff and dabbed at her eyes for a moment. Then to Garth's amazement, a change occurred on the old woman's countenance. Her eyes narrowed as her lips drew into a disapproving line. "Well, I made no such promise to her. I shall ring such a peal over that young lady she won't long forget."

Garth smiled. "I am certain you shall. Do not fret, between us, we shall manage to keep Lady Rose from disaster."

The woman gathered the remaining biscuits from the floor and tossed them into the refuse bin nearby. "Thank you for telling me, Mr. Sterling."

He rose, helping the woman to stand. He looked at the scant rations on the tray. "I shall go and distract Cook and Meg. Do find something a bit more nourishing than biscuits and plums. There is ham and cold chicken in the larder for when the gentlemen return this afternoon. No one will miss a few slices."

Garth opened the door and was about to depart when Benson called him.

"Since you know the truth, could I ask one other favor, Mr. Sterling?"

"Whatever you need." He quirked a dark brow.

A sheepish grin appeared on her lined face. "Candles. I'm too old to be sneaking about filching them from the wall braces, and we need them since nighttime is the only time her ladyship can safely rise. She's a restless one and will not stay abed as she should."

A dawning expression lit Garth's face. "So you were my candle thief!" He'd nearly accused Thomas of stealing. He'd have to allow the footman off early this evening since he couldn't apologize without explaining what had been happening to the candles. "I shall bring you a supply this evening after the other servants are retired." He knew it would give him an opportunity to add his words of disapproval to the young lady's adventures the previous night. As he made his way to where Cook and the maid were scrubbing turnips in the washroom the memory of Lady Rose in his arms the previous night returned. She'd been a delightful armful, but a decided distraction. His mission today was to get into Wingate's room and finish his search.

Over the course of the next three days, Garth found his effort to find the chalice thwarted. The young lord had come down with a mild cold and rarely left his room. Unable to fully search Lord Wingate's private apartments, Garth managed to explore each of the rooms closest at hand, thinking that the gentleman might have stowed the chalice somewhere safe from the prying hands of a cleaning servant. The furniture in the unused rooms were under Holland covers and from the amount of dust, it was clear they had not been disturbed in some time. Still, he made a cursory search in the cabinets and wardrobes. The chalice remained elusive.

Even as his pursuit of his family's treasure continued, his thoughts repeatedly returned to the young lady who was hiding out in her rooms. Boredom was the worst enemy of the young and that might prove dangerous if she once again got the wanderlust. Every time she left her room the danger of her charade being exposed increased. What she needed was something to enliven her time so she would not be tempted to leave. But what did young ladies like to do? The normal things like sewing and watercolors were probably not options for an active young woman like Lady Rose.

An idea came to him when he came across a book of pressed flowers in one of the cabinets he searched. Cook had told him about Lady Rose's love of gardening. He retrieved the volume, visited the garden to collect his specimens, waited until everyone in the household had retired, then paid a visit to her room.

His soft scratch on the door elicited silence, but after a long pause, Benson arrived at the door. She stepped back and gestured him in when she realized there was no danger. Ever cautious, she stepped into the hall and made certain no one had seen him before she closed the door.

Garth's gaze went to Lady Rose who played her role to the hilt. She lay still with her eyes closed, the very image of an unconscious woman. "Good evening, ladies."

Her eyes flew open and she sat up and eyed him hesitantly. "Good evening, Sterling. Benson tells me I owe you an apology for dragging you into my little adventure the other night." She looked shyly down at her blanket, then back at him. "I didn't think of what would have happened to you had father discovered us."

"You did your best to discourage me from going, my lady."

She grinned wickedly at him. "So I did and rather rudely as I remember. Pray forgive me."

He bowed his head slightly in a gesture he'd often seen his own family butler use. "It is forgotten, my lady."

"What brings you to the sickroom?" Her curious gaze had moved to what he was hiding behind his back.

Distracted by the sight of her with her blond hair tumbling from beneath her frilly white nightcap, and her night rail slipping off one shoulder, he had to force himself to concentrate on why he had come. "I found this today and thought you might like to see it." He handed her the leather-bound book and took note of a wistful smile as she ran her fingers over the raised floral design. He then pulled several blue blossoms from behind his back. "And to add another specimen to your collection. I fear I am unfamiliar with what this flower is called but I can find a book in the library that would help you categorize the variety."

She smiled and nearly took his breath away. "This

is wonderful, Sterling. I believe it is a larkspur, but a book would be just the thing."

The pair exchanged a smile, and Benson looked thoughtfully from one to the other. There seemed to be something electric in the air between them. When Sterling leaned over to look at a bud that Lady Rose was explaining, the old woman thought they made a striking couple, him so dark and her so fair—and the image jolted her. Such a thing was not to be considered. Their stations in life were too far apart.

The old woman hurried over and under her breath, said, "May I have a word with you outside, Mr. Sterling?"

The butler excused himself to Rose and promised a new bloom on the following night. He followed Nurse out into the hallway. "What can I do for you, Mrs. Benson?"

She shifted uncomfortably, for he was her superior in the household. "I thought perhaps I should warn you that young girls can be quite susceptible to the kindness of handsome young men—no matter their . . ." She didn't know how to politely warn him off.

Garth smiled. "No matter their ineligibility. You need have no fear that I will overstep my position. I merely brought the book to keep her amused while in her room." With that he bowed and left Benson.

Her gaze never left his well-shaped physique until he disappeared down the stairs. He seemed a likable young man and he could have little illusions that a hole-in-the-wall marriage would profit him in Lady Rose's case. His lordship spent too much time in Dun Territory and who better than his staff knew that.

Benson shook off her fears. No doubt it was this dreadful charade they were involved in that had her seeing villains behind every face. Sterling had proven his mettle the night he refused to let Lady Rose gallivant about on the moors alone. Only a man of honor would have risked his position with such a dangerous deed. On that thought she returned to find her young patient out of bed and poring over the old flower album. Why, Sterling had been right about the book distracting Lady Rose. Benson settled down to sleep certain that she wouldn't have to worry about the girl that night.

For Rose, Sterling's gesture had been endearing. Instead of pressing the larkspurs into one of the empty pages, she secreted them under her pillow. It had not been a courting gesture, but still it meant something that he'd thought about her enough to have gone and picked the blooms. She was quite unused to any man being so thoughtful.

By the end of the week, the York races came to an end and slowly most of the gentlemen who had come to purchase horses took their leave and returned to London. Only Robert's friend, Sir Marcus, remained, greatly lightening the work for his lordship's harried staff.

What worried Garth the most was that Lord Wingate, too, might return to London and take the chalice with him. However, with his friend in residence, he could hardly do so and Sir Marcus seemed quite content in Yorkshire. One look at the worn shirts that Thomas brought down to launder for the baronet made Garth suspect the foppish man's pockets were in much the same condition as Wingate's. Likely he was perfectly content to rusticate at someone else's expense.

A KISS AT MIDNIGHT 111

On the matter of Lady Rose, Garth heeded Benson's words. He had a fine line to tread. He came each night with a new flower, but he was polite and remote as his position demanded. She seemed content to remain sequestered and took each new bloom with eager delight. As to that daring ride on the moors, he could only hope that she had learned her lesson and would not soon repeat such a foolish stunt. Not only her health, but her future depended on her staying put in her room.

On Monday afternoon, things took a decided turn in Garth's favor when his lordship summoned him to the library.

"Ah, Sterling," his lordship looked up from a ledger in which he'd been inscribing numbers, his face relaxed in a smug smile. "I have been invited to Lord Godolphin's estate for a private sale of yearlings this week. I shall be gone until Friday next."

Even Garth, who did not follow the racing news, was well aware of what an honor it was to be included in the private sale of the famous Godolphin line of Arabians. Clearly the marquess' luck had held during the races if he could afford the purchase of such prime stock.

Denham put down his pen, and sat back. His mouth firmed to a hard line. "If Cherrington arrives this week, tell him nothing about Lady Rose and keep him away from her room. Propriety and all that balderdash. I'm to be summoned at once, and whatever you must do, don't allow the earl to leave, is that understood?"

"My lord, do you not think it best Lord Wingate be on hand to entertain the earl?" Garth was determined to do all in his power to keep the young man in Yorkshire.

"Wingate and his friend departed this morning for a mill halfway across country. It's a great lot of nonsense to be dashing off that far for a boxing match but there is some nonsense about it being the Black Ajax who fights. You must see to Cherrington, Sterling."

"Very good, my lord." The only way Garth wanted to deal with the old earl was to plant him a facer, but until he had the chalice in his hands he could not allow himself such a treat. He didn't lament the fact for long, because the marquess' news meant he would no longer be so encumbered with his duties. Wingate was not likely to haul the Fenton chalice to a prizefight. It would be far too cumbersome to hide in a phaeton.

It was all Garth could do not to rub his hands together with satisfaction. With both father and son gone, the house would be his to search from top to bottom. If the chalice were here, he should be able to find it in the next few days.

About to depart, a thought occurred to Garth. "My lord, since there will be no one to serve, might I allow the servants several days of their own?" Fewer people to question his extensive search. Even more so, they deserved the time after being utterly overworked for the past week. At his estate at Hillcrest, there would have been thrice the staff to handle so many.

A scowl returned to Lord Denham's face. "Do as you wish, Sterling, as long as they understand any free time is without pay and they are to be back at their posts on my return."

Garth kept his face impassive, but his thoughts condemned his lordship for his parsimonious ways. He bowed and was about to depart when his lordship stopped him.

"Whatever the others do, I shall need you here, Sterling. I placed several orders while I was in town and they should be delivered sometime this week."

"As you wish, my lord." Garth suspected the marquess had settled his accounts at the wine merchant, for the cellars were nearly empty. Strange that he had not given the task to Garth, but Denham was a man of sudden impulse, which too often hurt him at the races.

Garth headed straight to the servants' hall to inform Cook, Meg, Nell, and Thomas they would be allowed a respite after all their hard work. There was a great deal of excitement when Meg crowed with delight. She informed those gathered round the kitchen table that the Hiring Fair had come to York. While many servants came to such fairs to find new masters, most came for the entertainment at the events. Garth wasn't certain what would draw the marquess' staff, since they could certainly find a better master than Denham. But with the peace in France, jobs were scarce.

There was a great deal of discussion as the others gathered round to view the handbill that Meg pulled from her pocket. Such treats as lions, tigers, and monkeys were advertised along with plays, Punch's Family puppetry, and dancing cats and dogs. Both the younger girls announced their intention to travel to York, inviting Cook to join them. But the older woman declined. She preferred to visit her sister in Morley instead, not liking all the noise of fair crowds. Thomas gallantly offered to escort the young women, reminding them of the unruly behavior of many who visited the fair.

Meg smiled coquettishly up at Garth. "Do ye not wish to join us, Mr. Sterling? I can assure you the

Hiring Fairs are great fun." The little maid's eyes hinted that she would make certain of that and it would have little to do with wild animals and puppets.

Thomas, who very much liked the new butler since the man rarely criticized his visits to the tavern, added his voice to the invitation. "Chalmers often came with us to watch the boxing, Mr. Sterling. While it ain't the Ajax, it's grand sport. Lodgings are cheap in Coppergate during the fair. "

Garth had done his best to discourage Meg's romantic leanings so he addressed himself to the young footman. "Thank you, Thomas, but I shall stay here. His lordship did not give me leave to depart. You may all go and enjoy yourselves. Make certain that you are back by Thursday."

Only a momentary flash of disappointment showed on Meg's face, then she joined Thomas and Nell as they quickly dispersed, their excited babbling echoing in the servants' hall as they made their way to their rooms. They had to hurry to make the Mail coach for York that night which stopped at the local posting inn. Cook informed Garth that she would take the morning stage to visit her sister, which would give her time to prepare some food to leave for those who remained behind, but if he had a need for anything special Benson was quite capable if she could be coaxed away from Lady Rose's bedside. Cook declared it was such a shame about the young lady, then the woman set to work.

After seeing his lordship safely off, Garth returned to the task of making certain the furniture in the guest rooms were again covered while he awaited nightfall when he might search with little fear of discovery. He was more confident than he'd been since his arrival that he would soon have the chalice back in his hands. He could end this foolish masquerade and return to his own affairs at Hillcrest.

What then of Lady Rose and her whole dilemma? He tried to tell himself she was none of his concern. Yet his thoughts returned to the feeling of holding her in his arms as he'd brought her back to the estate after her madcap ride. He gripped the edge of the desk, irritated by the distraction. He was not some green lad.

Determined to put the girl from his mind, he pulled open a cabinet in the hall and began searching through the linens to see if Lord Wingate might have been foolish enough to store the chalice there. Lady Rose was an enterprising young lady and likely would manage to slip the matrimonial noose that Cherrington was trying to tighten. Garth had his own affairs to tend.

"Everyone is leaving?" Rose sat up in bed without the least dizziness. She had been a dutiful patient since Benson had read her the riot act about her ride on the moors and her nightly visits from Sterling. She looked forward to each new flower, surely it had nothing to do with the handsome butler.

Sleeping, reading, and her flower book had become her primary occupation and she was utterly sick of such pastimes. The only bright spots to her nights were Sterling's visit and since the first night he'd become quite remote, seeming to put up a wall between them.

Pushing the handsome butler from her mind, her thoughts returned to her boredom. She was fully recovered from her injury, no longer experiencing any odd effects, like the dizziness which had plagued her in the beginning when she moved about. There was little doubt that she rode on the moors before she was fully recovered. But she had been days without any symptoms, not even the slightest headache. She wished there was something she could safely do that was outside this cursed room and this was surely her opportunity with everyone gone.

Benson stood at the rosewood chest of drawers putting away the clean night rails that she'd just washed and ironed. "The young gentlemen decamped early and his lordship after nuncheon. Cook said the servants hied off for York before supper. She leaves in the morning to visit her sister. That means you and I, and, of course, Mr. Sterling, shall be quite on our own."

Rose tossed back the covers and dropped her feet over the side of the bed while a world of possibilities danced in her head. There would be no one to see her, at least over the course of the next week, which meant she could be free from this gilded cage.

"And just what are you plotting, my lady?"

Benson stood at the foot of the bed with arms akimbo, glaring at her young charge.

"Don't you see, Benny? I shan't have to stay hidden in this room since there won't be anyone save Sterling about, and he already knows my secret." A blush warmed her cheeks as she remembered her nurse's reprimand that Rose had not only endangered Benson's position but Sterling's as well.

"Do you want to risk being seen by some unexpected caller or the gardener or one of the grooms? You dare not take the chance, my lady."

Rose, in her eagerness to be out of her room, hadn't considered such possibilities. Denham Hall, like many Jacobean manors, possessed great walls of windows in the drawing rooms, library, and most of the ground floor apartments. Curtains or closures of any kind were rarely used to block out the light. Were she to visit one of the rooms she would be visible to anyone in the gardens. She slid from the bed and went to the window and drew back the curtains. The sun had set and the last gleam of light was rapidly fading on the western horizon. She had done her best to behave as Benny wished, but her patience was wearing thin. She simply could not miss this opportunity. But how to convince her old nurse there was no danger at night?

A smile touched her mouth when an idea came to her. She wandered casually to the fireplace and slumped down into a chair, then uttered a great sigh. "I begin to think I *should* leave Denham Hall, Benny. We both know that I shall not last another fortnight isolated here from everything and everyone. This escapade is doomed to failure."

The old woman's eyes widened. "Do not say such, my lady. You have no place to go and there is too much that could happen to a proper young lady who hasn't the least idea how to manage on her own. Could you not consider Lord Cherrington?"

"Never!" Rose shuddered.

"Then I do not know what to suggest. I can think of no other safe alternatives," Benson fretted.

Rose watched Nurse carefully and was convinced she needed only a bit more to sway the woman into allowing her, at the very least, to venture from this accursed room at night. "Only think, if I must leave Denham, it should be at once while Father and Robert are away from home. I would have nearly a full week to make my escape before they were even aware I had gone."

Benson came and stood before the girl. "Stop this nonsense at once. You cannot leave the Hall." Her gaze searched Lady Rose's face, then she crossed her arms. "I think this is all a hum, my dear girl. You are trying to frighten me into letting you go outside. Well, the best you can hope for is to be allowed downstairs, but not outdoors. Is that understood?" Receiving a nod, she added, " I want no more talk of you leaving, is that understood?"

Rose could never fool Benson. She hugged the woman. "I promise I won't go out during the day when the grooms and gardener are about. I just need to free myself from this small space if only for a few hours."

Benson settled in a chair, certain she was being cozened, but with a lingering fear that Lady Rose might yet try to leave. "Go child. Wander about to your heart's content. Cook will be in her room by now as will Sterling."

Excited, Rose dashed to her wardrobe and pulled out a white muslin and lace wrapper trimmed with pink ribbons. She was as giddy as a girl at her first ball as she opened the door to her room and stepped into the hallway. Her lone candle lit only a small circle around her, leaving both ends of the hallway in darkness. Sweet freedom.

Then a rush of guilt washed over her. She should not have frightened Benny with threats of leaving, but she had become desperate. Between Nurse and Sterling they were determined to wrap her in cotton wool. They both didn't seem to understand that three years away at school had done much to foster her self-reliance. There had been no loyal servants there to protect her when she and her friends had stumbled across a band of Irish Travelers in the woods. Only Rose's stubborn nature and a sturdy limb had saved them. The experience had taught her not to give way to fear and that she could succeed.

A strange thumping sound echoed at the East end of the hallway. Rose listened for a moment thinking it was her imagination, then she heard it again. It appeared to be coming from the direction of Robert's room. Had her brother returned home? That seemed highly unlikely but perhaps something had happened that had forced the men to give up their plans.

The tapping continued at short intervals and Rose's curiosity got the better of her. She slipped down the hallway and listened at Robert's door. The sound emanated from behind the door and a bit of light came from under the oak portal, reflecting off her white satin bed slippers.

Clearly Robert was up to something, or why else had he returned in such a clandestine manner after their father was gone. That gave Rose an idea. The tables would be balanced. She wouldn't tell their father about what Robert was up to if he didn't tell about her. An ally might be nice and she might even be able to coax her brother into taking her riding at night for she did so long to go outdoors again. Sterling couldn't object if Robert went along on a midnight ride. A strange weakness came to her knees as memories of her midnight ride with the butler returned, his strong hands as he'd lifted her and the safety of his arms round her.

Realizing such thoughts were dangerous, she straightened. Sterling was her friend only, just like Chalmers. Taking a deep breath, she opened the door to her brother's room without making a sound and peered into the dimly lit interior.

To her complete dismay she found the man who'd just dominated her thoughts standing at the wall tapping at the wainscoting in search of heaven knew what.

"Sterling, what are you doing in my brother's room?"

The butler turned in surprise, but with only a slight hesitation said, "Oh, Lord Wingate thinks he has rats in his walls, my lady."

Rose recoiled at the thought. Her father had allowed the manor to get rather shabby over the last few years but they had not quite sunk so low as to have rats, had they? "Have you seen any?"

"No, my lady. I suspect he imagined them while in his cups."

That was a relief to Rose, but before she could comment, the butler came to where she stood in the doorway. Combined light from both their candles allowed her to more clearly see the expression on his face, and he didn't look well pleased to see her. He towered over her, making her feel small and vulnerable. His gaze swept her wrapper and the frown on his face relaxed.

"Am I right in assuming you do not intend to take to the moors tonight, my lady?"

Anger warmed Rose's cheeks and she turned on her heel, saying over her shoulder, "That is none of your concern, Sterling. I think you forget yourself. What I do is none of your affair." She strode down the hall, but she was not to escape his presence. Within minutes he was again at her side.

"There you are completely wrong, my lady." There was steel in his tone.

Rose stopped and looked up into his blue eyes and a wave of unfamiliar emotion shimmered inside her. Just when she thought him her friend, he again behaved in the most highhanded manner. She had to struggle to manage the proper indignation which sounded weak even to her ears. "How dare you. You are my father's butler. That does not allow you to command me in my father's house."

A soft chuckle escaped him. "You set the rules of the game, my lady. When you cozened that promise to remain silent, I was left as one of two who might make you see reason. What do you think would have happened had you been alone on the moors that night when you had a dizzy spell?"

She looked away from him. Even she could not deny that she might have collapsed on the road and been unable to return home safely. Then all she had endured would have been for naught. It didn't bear thinking about. "I am better now. I am safe inside the house and there is no need for you to bother about me further. Return to your rat-catching."

Without another word she marched off toward the head of the stairs. She hurried down the marble steps and when she reached the bottom, to her chagrin, he again stepped into her path. A wicked grin tipped his mouth when she glared up at him. "What do you think you are doing? I told you I am none of your concern."

"But you are my concern when you are out of that room, Lady Rose."

She was being utterly childish without doubt, but his very nearness seemed to sap her reason. "If you do not go away, I'll . . . I'll . . ."

"You'll tell your father." His grin grew wider, making him even more appealing. "Face your fate, my lady. You are quite stuck with me as your guardian during your nocturnal excursions."

Rose would not stamp her foot in frustration, she had not forgotten herself that much, but she was torn. On the one hand she didn't want him there prosing on about what she could and could not do. Still there was a thrill at the thought that she would have such an appealing companion for she could not deny that during her long nights she'd been lonely. Here was a companion who made her pulse race and made her feel alive, which days and days in her rooms had robbed her. Why, moving about in the spectral light of her candle made her seem already dead and buried here at Denham. What a foolish thought! She looked up into those eyes that seemed to miss nothing.

"Oh, very well. I am going to the library to choose some books that are more to my liking than the battles and sermons that Benny has been bringing me. If you think I shall be attacked by brigands there, come along."

Without another word, she headed straight for her father's library.

Garth stood for a moment, a wave of relief washing over him while he watched her shapely figure disappear down the rear hall. Not only was she beautiful, but she had a quick mind. How he managed to fool her in Wingate's room with that far-fetched tale about rats, he didn't know. He only thanked God for females' universal revulsion to rodents. That had been quite a close thing.

When she disappeared into the library, he realized her nightclothes were a mixed blessing. They told him she did not intend to leave the Hall that night which greatly relieved his mind, but seeing her in *de-*

shabille, her golden curls tumbling from beneath her frilly night cap, did little to dampen his growing fascination with the chit.

The temptation to leave her to her own devices burgeoned at the back of his mind. She was a distraction he didn't need tonight. But Lady Rose was too unpredictable to allow to wander loose. He might next find her traipsing about the gardens in her flimsy attire. She seemed to have no sense of danger, the innocent little minx. His conscience wouldn't allow him to abandon her to her whims though.

He followed her into the large book-lined room. She had pulled several small volumes from the stacks. It was patently obvious that she was deliberately ignoring him since she kept her back to him. Amused, he relaxed against the doorjamb and waited to see what she would do next. After flipping through several more volumes, she picked up her selections and moved back toward him.

"If you insist on being my shadow, at least make yourself useful." She shoved the dusty volumes into his hand, then went into the hall, headed toward the kitchen. He followed her at a leisurely pace, convinced for the present that she was not likely to get into trouble.

The warm smell of baked bread still lingered in the kitchens where Cook had prepared several days' worth for those who remained at the estate. There was a lantern lit beside the fireplace and the candle the lady had carried sitting on the kitchen table. Yet Lady Rose was nowhere to be seen. Then a clatter of crockery in the pantry and she stepped into the main room with a covered tray and a pitcher of milk.

Retrieving a glass from the hutch, she poured herself some milk, then took a small poppy seed cake from the tray. She offered him one, which he refused, then with a shrug of her shoulders, she took a bite from the cake, then sat down at the table. A crumpled piece of paper caught her attention and she picked it up and turned the sheet toward the light to read.

Garth's heart sank as he recognized the handbill Meg had left behind. His gaze never left her but he could see the growing excitement light her face. Her eyes sparkled as she looked up at him. "The Hiring Fair is in York?"

"It is, my lady. I hope you are not thinking about going."

A shuttered look came to her face. "I merely asked a question."

Garth was not fooled. It was written all over her face that she wanted to go. And she could have little doubt that he would try and stop her, so she denied her interest. In a flash of insight he sensed she would try to slip out on her own and she might well succeed. He couldn't sit guard outside her room day and night for the next week. Even with Benson keeping watch, the ingenious girl could very likely slip away, and to what danger? Forbidding her to go was pointless. There was only one thing he could do. It was a risk, but it would ensure she was not unprotected during her visit.

"Can you contrive a suitable disguise, Lady Rose?"

Her brows shot up. "A disguise?"

"If I were to take you to the Hiring Fair tomorrow night, could you manage a suitable costume? One that is good enough that even a close friend would not recognize you?"

She bounded to her feet. "I can create such a disguise. Do you truly mean to take me to York?"

All his reservations melted in the face of her eager delight. "I do."

"And you won't object to my seeing everything?" Her wide smile warmed his heart.

"You may see everything you desire, that is, until midnight. Then we must return here."

Garth was aware of the risk he was taking. Yet as he looked at the gleam in her lovely green eyes, he didn't care about risk. He would face the consequences should they be discovered.

"Oh, thank you, Sterling." In her excitement, she rushed round the table and threw her arms round him. "You are truly a friend."

The feel of her soft femininity pressed against him caused a rush of desire and his arms closed round her instinctively. Friendship did not describe the feeling he experienced at that moment. Garth straightened as he realized what he was about. She was an innocent young girl. He took her arms from his neck and put her from him. "Be ready by dark, my lady."

She stared at him with bewilderment for a moment. When a blush appeared on her cheeks, he suspected she was appalled that she'd been so familiar with a servant. She turned her head away, too embarrassed to look at him. "I will be ready, Sterling."

Without another word, she grabbed up her books and left the kitchen. Garth wondered if he were an utter fool to risk his search for this young woman. Yet when he thought of what her future might hold, the risk seemed a small thing.

Seven

Rose shrugged into the musty jacket that Benny had found in the attic inside a cabinet full of Robert's old clothes. The green damask waistcoat and beige breeches were a bit too large, but that only helped to cover her feminine curves. She was still surprised that Sterling had agreed to take her to York. Also that he had convinced her nurse no harm would come of such an adventure. Although his promises to have her home safely by midnight had done little to alleviate Benny's worries. Her old nurse only relented because he'd suggested that one night at the fair would buy her Rose's obedience for the next month. Rose had grudgingly agreed to such a bargain, hoping that Lord Cherrington would soon be a bad memory and her self-imposed exile would end much sooner than thirty days.

After fastening the last brass button on the brown coat, Rose went to the mirror to inspect her disguise. Benny had tightly braided her hair, then pinned it in a neat corona high atop her head. A grin lit her face at the sight of what appeared a slender, unshaven youth of no more than sixteen.

The door to her room opened and Benson entered, carrying a black hat with oversized brim. "I found this in a box of . . ." The woman paused, her brows drawing together at the sight of Rose. "Again I must say I cannot like you going as a lad, my lady. 'Tis rather indecent to be exposing your limbs in such a manner."

Rose smoothed the fabric of her coat. "'Tis not the first time I've donned such a costume Benny."

"And look what came of that. You got yourself sent away to school. You should not do this. The fair is no place for a lady."

"That is why I must go as a man. Besides, Sterling will be there. He is a rather imposing figure of a man." She certainly couldn't deny that he affected her each time she saw him anew.

"Humph, it's his judgment I'm more concerned with. Like I said before, he's far too young to be a proper butler. But I think he will manage this, for he has the brawn."

While Rose had only briefly attended a sheep fair and not one like this, she'd heard tales from the maids. Fairs drew a bawdy crowd and females attended at their own risk.

Nurse's mouth puckered into a disapproving moue but she handed the hat to the young lady despite her apprehension. Rose tugged it over her golden hair, removing the last hint of her feminine gender. She would not be able to take her hat off, but there would be no need in the rough company they were about to enter.

"Promise you will not leave Mr. Sterling's side, my lady. York is a very large city and one could be lost for days in those narrow streets."

Rose laughed. "You sound as if I have never been there before, dear Benny." Seeing the worried look deepen on Nurse's face, she added more seriously, "I won't get lost and I won't leave Sterling's side. I promise."

"Things look very different in the dark amid the crush of a crowd, child. Already I'm regretting agreeing to this nonsense." The old woman shook her head and sank into a nearby chair. "I can feel it in my bones that nothing good will come of this night."

Rose swept the hat from her head and knelt beside the old woman's chair. "'Tis only the fair we go to, Benny, not to war. I shall walk around, view the sights, sample some of the food, and then Sterling will see me safely home." She patted the old woman's hand. "I do not know how this charade we play shall end, but if my father succeeds and eventually forces me to marry some gentleman I do not love, I wish to always have this last moment of freedom to cherish."

Benny kissed her charge atop her head. "Oh, don't listen to me, child. I am an old woman who worries too much. Stay with Sterling and all will be well."

Having Benny's blessing was like getting final absolution for a grievous sin. Rose bounded to her feet, eager to be on her way. She tugged her hat on then hurried to her dresser and found the few coins she'd saved over the past few years. "I shall bring you a present, Benny."

The woman gave something between a sniffle and a chuckle. "The only present I want, child, is you home safe."

After further assurances Rose took her leave of Nurse, urging her to get some rest. Then she hurried down to the front hall, which she found empty. She paced nervously in front of the double doors, waiting on Sterling. Had he changed his mind? She didn't think so, but where could he be? Chasing rats again? She laughed at such a foolish notion, then stepped to the mirror and tugged her hat a bit forward so that her face was in shadow. Even if she were to meet one of her old friends from the neighborhood, no one would know her. The clandestine nature of this only added to the fun in Rose's mind.

As the ormolu clock on the mantelpiece ticked closer to seven, Rose grew more anxious. She stepped to the front door and tugged it open. The evening sky was growing dark. Surely they should be on their way.

The sound of footsteps on the marble floor alerted her that Sterling was ready. She turned to see him coming toward her down the hall and a tiny gasp escaped her. He'd changed from his black butler's rig to a well-worn blue coat over a tan waistcoat and tan breeches. Except for the heavy brown brogans and navy stocking he wore, she might have mistaken him for a gentleman. She knew a brief moment of regret that they would never be considered equals, then she pushed it away. Tonight was for enjoyment and not laments.

He halted at the end of the staircase when he spotted her standing in the doorway. A frown came on his brow, and there was no recognition in his eyes. "May I help . . ." he started to say, then he realized who she was. "Lady Rose?" His expression darkened. "When I suggested a disguise I was thinking of a farmer's wife or chamber maid, not a male."

His gaze raked her and Rose experienced a strange quiver in her limbs. This was dangerous ground, and she didn't want to miss her opportunity to go to the fair. "We, er, Benson thought I would be less likely to be recognized as a lad than as a young woman." She tamped down the guilt at prevaricating such a plumper. Benson had been no happier with her disguise than Sterling.

He stood in silence, his gaze again sweeping her from head to toe. A strange look settled in his eyes, and he turned away. "Perhaps you are correct. Shall we go?" He strode out the door and Rose followed in his path, eager for her night of entertainment.

Fairs were the only true amusement the *hoi polloi* of England enjoyed. They were brash, boisterous, and earthy affairs that never seemed to cease their calamitous activity from morn till night. York's Hiring Fair sprang up twice a year in the early summer and late autumn without any true planning or management. It simply seemed to appear one day along with tumblers, clowns, jugglers, rhymesters, and musicians who traveled the roads much of the year from sheep fairs to horse fairs or any fair where they could earn their keep.

Like most young men, Garth had experienced his rite of passage and visited the local fair near Hillcrest in his youth. To his youthful eyes it had been exciting and fun, but now as he stared down Parliament Street in York with Lady Rose at his side, the mass of milling people appeared vulgar and raucous. He questioned his decision to bring her, but he hadn't been willing to risk her sneaking out to come without a chaperone.

Above the din he said, "Watch out for pickpockets in this crush."

Lady Rose showed not the least trepidation. She tugged at his jacket. "What shall we see first, Sterling?"

Garth scanned the various stalls along the street. He searched for something appropriate for a delicately bred female. From the peepshows to the dancing female revues, there seemed to be little.

They would need to go deeper into the chaos. "Shall we walk further down the street and find the wild animal cages?"

"Do they have lions and monkeys?" Her eyes widened and she took in everything, showing not the least bit of shock.

"Very likely." Garth couldn't resist her excitement. They moved deeper into the teeming mass of gaiety and a broader variety of vendors hawked their wares. First, Rose bought several sweetmeats to take to Benson. They watched an organ grinder and his dancing monkey dressed like a clown move about in the crowd, extending his cup after each silly dance. Garth began to relax and enjoy the experience. He was there to keep her safe and nothing was likely to go wrong.

They pushed their way through the throng, stopping to buy sausages from a spit then sweet rolls at the next stall. He purchased an entire bottle of cider, convincing her that the crockery was not so clean in shops that sold the sweet liquid by the cup.

"Look, Sterling, they have trained pets who do tricks. May we see them?" She pointed to a banner that fluttered in the wind with the figure of a man directing a group of cats and dogs to walk upright.

"I believe that is the reason we came, is it not?" He grinned at her, then led the way . He wound along the street at a steady pace. His imposing figure caused the crowd to part as he forged a path. Lady Rose followed in his wake, taking in all the sights and sounds.

While he looked for the arena, Garth caught sight of his brother coming straight at them, still dressed in his Yorkshire garb. Jack's eyes brightened on seeing his brother and he raise a hand in greeting.

Garth gave a slight shake of his head to warn his brother away. The young man stepped into a booth and watched them pass. He followed at a discrete distance. At last they made their way to the small arena where Garth stopped and pointed out a spot near the rail to Lady Rose. She slipped into the spot to await the show's start, all the while inspecting the other spectators who stood round the rail.

After several minutes, a stout woman wearing a bright yellow muslin gown that over-exposed her ample charms, stepped out and announced the show was about to begin. People moving along the street stopped and gathered round the wood rails. Presently the curtain on the small stage shook and a thin man in a garish purple suit of clothes from another century stepped into the arena. He was followed by two eager black spaniels and a spotted terrier. The dogs all danced along on their hind feet, front paws held in front of them and a roar of approval went up from the crowd. A young boy, wearing a dirty, red skeleton suit, carried two small painted barrels out to the center of the arena—then he returned behind the curtain and reappeared with a small ladder which he set up on the barrels.

After the show got under way and Lady Rose was duly absorbed, Garth slipped across the street to where Jack waited.

"Who's the lad?" The younger Fenton gestured with a jerk of his head as he continued to scan the faces in the crowd, fearful of being seen by one of his fashionable friends who might be in York.

Garth smiled, never taking his gaze from his charge. "Lady Rosamund."

Jack head swivelled back toward the figure at the rail. He couldn't help but gawk at a proper miss in breeches. "Have you taken leave of your senses, Garth? If Denham were to learn you brought his daughter to this Gomorrah, you might find yourself with a wife."

"Not very likely, dear brother. The marquess has richer game in sight for the young lady. But I had little choice. She is quite determined. Once she heard about the fair, I knew she would try and come, with or without an escort. What have you learned about the jewels?"

Jack's gaze swept the girl's attire one last time; then he quirked a brow and shrugged. "I have only managed to visit a couple of shops and with no luck. No one has been offering to sell loose stones."

Garth frowned. It had been over four days since he'd last spoken with his brother. "What have you been doing with your time, if not looking for the jewels?"

The younger man shuffled his feet, and avoided looking his brother in the eye. "Some of these fair troubadours have been drinking at the inn and . . . they're an amusing lot, Garth. Got a bit diverted when old Becker tried to teach me to juggle. . . ."

Garth never felt more like throttling his brother than at that moment. "Don't get distracted again. We need to find out where Wingate might sell those jewels. There might be as many as twenty such places in a city the size of York and you have . . ."

"Eight in York proper. I asked a local pickpocket that I met . . ." Seeing the look on his brother's face, the young man changed the direction of the conversation. "Is it not possible that Robert has not even pried the stones from the Chalice yet? The first jeweler I visited said emeralds and rubies are easily damaged when removing them from fixed settings, not like diamonds."

Jostled by a passerby, Garth stepped aside, then returned to his brother's side. "You may be right. But I am more prone to think the need for the stones has not been pressing. The races have taken up much of his free time. I suppose that since he is residing at home and doesn't require the funds the stones would bring, he hasn't begun to vandalize the chalice as yet or"—he frowned—"he didn't bring the thing into Yorkshire in the first place."

The younger Fenton swore under his breath. "What will we do if he's got the cursed thing stashed in London?"

"He'd be a fool to try to sell those jewels in London. I'm convinced it's here somewhere and I shall find it. Have you written Father of our lack of progress?"

Jack declared he'd been too busy, then blushed when Garth eyed him doubtfully. It was soon decided they needed to keep the old gentleman informed. The two men discussed what Jack should tell their parents in a letter that would keep from upsetting their mother any further.

Across the crowded lane, Rose turned to ask Sterling if they might now find the wild animals. A tingle of fear raced down her spine when she discovered that he wasn't directly behind her. On tiptoe, she hurriedly searched the area. Then she spied him across the way in conversation with a young man in an old-fashioned frock coat. As she watched the two men, there was something vaguely similar in the way they held their heads when they spoke. Were they related? It occurred to her that she knew very little about the man who'd brought her to the fair and yet she still trusted him. How strange.

Something about the younger man drew her attention closer. There was a secretive quality to the way he kept looking up and down the street, as if fearful he might be seen, then he would lean toward Sterling and speak close to his ear. She could almost believe that the two men were up to something clandestine the way they conversed. Yet she could not envision Sterling being involved in something untoward. The intensity of the conversation made her uncomfortable about interrupting their discussion and she lingered where she was.

When the crowd around the arena began to disperse, Sterling looked to where she stood and their eyes locked. He immediately ceased speaking and gave a curt nod to the young man. He then crossed the lane to where she waited.

"Have you seen enough of dancing hounds?" He stepped between her and the departing young man, as if trying to keep her from getting a good look at the fellow.

"The show is ended. Did your friend give you bad news?"

"Friend?" Sterling's face went blank.

"The man with whom you were in such deep conversation."

He turned and surveyed a pair of pretty maids who passed by and giggled at him. Rose felt a flush of embarrassment when one of the girls winked at her. For a moment she'd forgotten how she was dressed. She scowled and Sterling must have taken the gesture as a reminder he hadn't answered her question.

In a casual voice, he said, "Oh, the lad. He was just someone who worked for my last employer. He stopped to tell me he has found a new post as well."

That seemed very strange to Rose for the conversation had seemed intense, almost angry at times. But then it was none of her affair whom he socialized with. He had no obligation to inform her what he did on his own time.

She fought to overlook the twinge of regret that thought caused her and began to search the crowded area for something else that would amuse her. They made their way down the street, stopping to watch a man juggle fire, and then a silly puppet show. At last they found the lion and tiger cages, but Rose was more appalled than delighted at the small, dirty carts that housed the animals, who lay listlessly on straw beds. Sterling quickly led her away, distracting her with several young lads who rode standing on the backs of plumed and bedecked Welsh ponies.

A clock over a shop in Parliament Street chimed the hour of ten and Rose realized her night at the fair was nearing an end. She searched the stalls for one last thing to end her adventure. Her eyes grew wide when she saw a fortune-telling tent at the next turn. "The Gypsies are here, I must have my fortune read."

Sterling's hand closed over her arm. "I don't think that a good idea. Those people are not to be trusted."

"Are you superstitious? Don't be silly, Sterling. It's all just great fun."

Before he could protest further, she pulled her arm free and hurried down the lane, weaving among the crowd until she came to Madame Suldana's tent. Did she truly want to know her future? Then she gave a laugh. Hadn't she said it was just great fun? Yet deep within, a tingle of trepidation nibbled at her at what she might learn about her future.

* * *

Madame Suldana jerked the partial deck of tarot cards out of her son's hands when she returned to the table after a visit to the necessary. He withheld one card. The remainder of the deck formed a tottering tower structure on the table.

"Give me those, *idióta*. These are our bread and butter not some toy for your witless amusement." Her husky voice still held a foreign lilt from her childhood in the Balkan Mountains.

"Ain't got no customers," Vitas said, his tones holding not a trace of accent since he had been born in the caravan twenty years ago while the Travelers moved from the Welsh Drover's Fair to the Devon Pony Fair. He placed the last card he held on the tower he'd constructed. He held his breath a moment as the structure wobbled, then held. He grinned with foolish delight. But his mother soon put a period to all his effort when she toppled the cards and gathered them into the deck.

Without warning, she slapped the oversized lad on the head, the silver trinkets and bangles on her arm jangling against his ear. "Get out front and bark my services. There's nothing in the caravan to eat save stale bread and no money to buy more. If you want to eat on the morrow you'll do your job."

Vitas grumbled that he was sorely used and far suited to better tasks, but fear of his mother's Gypsy temper made him lumber out of the chair to do as she bade him. He'd scarcely begun to shout of his mother's talent when a willowy lad came up inquiring about having his future told. He ushered the boy into the tent, then sauntered over to where they sold cheap libations and pork pies, knowing his mother would likely draw several coins from the silly fellow.

Inside the tent Madame gave a seductive smile to the slender youth who ducked into the tent. Age had dimmed her beauty but not her taste for appealing men, and the lad appeared decidedly handsome in the lantern light. He looked around curiously then sat in the chair that the fortune-teller gestured toward. "Come, do not fear the future, my fine young blade."

The Gypsy straightened the turban on her head, giving her time to inspect her prospective dupe. She surmised the clothes weren't cut for the lad, but clearly he was Quality. "What will you have, young sir? For a half-farthing Madame will read your palm, for a farthing I shall read your tarot cards," she fanned the deck onto the red cloth with a flourish. "Or for two farthings, madame can give you her best reading with her crystal ball." She gestured to a glass globe, which sat on a table in the rear of the tent surrounded by candles. It glowed eerily in the dim light, a trick of lighting her mother had taught her using a hole in the cloth and a small candle under the table.

The boy dug in his coat pocket. He put a half-farthing on the tablecloth. In a soft voice he said, "It shall have to be my palm, Madame. I cannot afford more."

All her hopes were dashed as she looked at the paltry coin. If he could not afford more than her least expensive reading, he was not likely to afford her more intimate services. She grabbed the money from the table and stuffed it into her leather pouch, then looked up at the young man and grinned. He smiled back and Madame frowned.

Pretty! That would best describe her young client.

The Gypsy peered closer at her patron, cursing the dim lighting. Something wasn't right about the lad who sat with his hat pulled down casting his face in shadow, but exactly what she couldn't quite put her finger on. She doubted youth gave him the dainty traits that struck such a strange quality on a young man. The woman might not have the true gift of foresight, but she was wise to the ways of the world. Something was definitely havey-cavey here.

With a deep sigh of puzzlement, Madame began her flamboyant routine. Her bangles clattered when she reached across the table. "Give me your hand and Madame Suldana will tell you all the good luck that you may enjoy."

There was a moment's hesitation, then a slender white hand was extended to the fortune-teller. The moment Madame touched her customer, a prickle of cognizance raced through her. What young man would have such soft, delicate hands? Even the most foppish of her customers possessed hands that, while well-maintained, were lean and sinewy with a growth of wiry hair. This little hand was smooth and well-shaped with tapered finger nails.

Madame's gaze flew to her client's face. This time she looked closer at the heart-shaped countenance beneath the oversized hat. Flawless skin, delicately arched brows, and full rose-bud lips told the true tale. Very likely the girl was older than she looked and certainly she should not be at a Hiring Fair near midnight. Madame turned the girl's hand palm up, wondering if this knowledge might benefit her and Vitas in some way. What would this girl pay to keep her family from knowing about her visit to the fair? Clearly she had few funds with her but Quality was hard to disguise and caution rather than pockets to let probably accounted for her lack of money. There were always ways to get money from people who lived in large houses. The only question that remained was where the girl came from and would there be wealth enough to flow into Suldana's pockets?

She peered intently at the girl's extended palm. "Madame sees a very long life for you." The Gypsy traced her finger along the girl's lifeline. Then she bent closer as if seeing something of importance. "Ah, I see you have many secrets in your life, dear boy."

"Do you?" There was awe with a hint of fear in the girl's voice.

"There is something that you do not wish your father to know. Something very important." Madame watched the girl's eyes go wide and knew she'd struck gold. "You must be very careful or your secrets will be revealed."

The girl gasped. "What must I do?"

"You will know what to do when the need arises. Remember, there is always a price to pay to keep such a secret." *More than you will know, dear girl,* Madame mused.

With a befuddled shake of her head, the young lady hesitantly asked, "Do you see . . . a marriage in my future?"

Madame pulled the girl's hand closer as if reinspecting the lines. It was fortunate that she'd realized her patron a female, for what she told women always involved love and marriage, while for men she predicted fortune and adventure. "I do see marriage in your future and very soon." She leaned even closer, driving home her point. "A person of title, I think. Money shall be no object to your fondest wishes and . . ."

Before she could finish her traditional speech the pretend lad stood up and pulled her hand free. "I must go." The young lady in breeches practically flew from the tent.

Madame lifted her colorful skirts and followed the girl out the door. She grabbed Vitas by the ear yanking him from a barrel where he sat drinking a tankard of Blue Ruin.

"Hurry, *fajankó*, and follow that girl!"

Vitas wiped his mouth on his sleeve, and peered round for a female in the thinning throng. "What female?"

"That one, in the breeches with the oversized black hat." Madame pointed after the lad who'd joined another man.

"Yer daft, *Anyu*. That ain't no female." He peered at the lad.

"Aye, 'tis a female and one very likely to be our fortune. Follow her. I want to know where she lives and who she is."

Still doubtful, Vitas grunted then took a final gulp of Ruin. At his delay, his mother whacked him on the head. "Get moving, *fiú*. I don't want to lose our golden goose."

Rose raced away from the fortune-teller's tent and ran straight into Sterling who stood watching two clowns flirt with a pretty serving wench from the local ale house. The words "a titled gentleman" rang in her ears, over and over. She would have staggered blindly into the crowd had he not reached out and grabbed her shoulders. "Steady there. What is wrong?"

"I wish to go home." A tightening in her throat almost kept the words from coming out.

His gaze raked her face and his mouth went taut, but to Rose's relief he asked no questions. "Very well."

They made their way back along the street but Rose saw nothing in her daze of anguish. All the while the Gypsy's revelations whirled round and round in Rose's mind. Was the woman a charlatan or did she have true powers of foresight? How had she known Rose had a secret? Was that not proof the Gypsy was a true fortune-teller? How could Rose doubt that Madame's prediction of a marriage to a titled gentleman would not come true? She had not asked for the gentleman's name, for it would only have made the prediction more unbearable to hear. There was only one titled gentleman of her acquaintance who aspired to her hand. A wave of nausea washed over Rose.

At last they reached the inn where they had left the hired gig. Rose stumbled as she climbed into the small vehicle, and a strong hand gripped her arm. With Sterling's help she righted herself and took her seat.

"Are you ill, my lady?" Sterling asked as he watched her settle onto the worn leather seat of the Brown Pigeon's gig.

She could see the concern in his eyes, and she made an attempt to smile. "Only a bit tired. Shall we go? I am certain that Benson will not sleep until we return." Rose took a deep breath and the sick feeling began to subside.

He made no comment, only stared at her a moment longer, then climbed into the gig. He urged the old horse out into the street heading toward Denham Hall. Within ten minutes they had left behind the lights of York, but after that Sterling kept the horse at a slow steady pace due to the darkness and his unfamiliarity with the road.

Free from the curious eyes of strangers, Rose pulled the hat from her head and tugged the braid free from its pins, convinced that was what made her head hurt. She leaned back in the seat and stared up at the moon shrouded in a thick corona but there was no joy in the lovely sight. She wished she had heeded Sterling and not visited Madame Suldana—not had her hopes destroyed. It made her wonder what he knew that she did not.

Her gaze moved to his strong profile. "Do you think that people have the power to foretell the future?"

He shrugged. "Some people think so. The Scottish have a word to describe such people. They are called *fey*. But I don't believe that Madame Suldana is anything but a cheat."

"Why do you think her false?" Rose asked, but a heavy weight of despair had taken hold of her outside the Gypsy's tent and she couldn't seemed to shake free of its icy grip.

"If such a woman possessed true powers of foresight, do you not think she would be wealthy and much feted by those who sought her services?" He was silent for a moment then asked, "What did she foretell for you?"

Rose sighed. "What does it matter, if you say she does not possess any gift of insight?"

The dejection in her voice was almost palpable and he pressed her. "Shall I guess what she said?"

Rose was silent. He was trying to make her see reason, to show her the silliness of such people, but he did not know all that the woman had been able to discern.

"Let me guess. She predicted either that you were

going to come into a great fortune, go on a great journey or . . . marry very well."

Rose gasped at his accuracy. She peered closer at his handsome silhouette against the moonlit sky. Again she regretted that he was considered beneath her touch for she was rapidly gaining a great deal of respect for him. "How did you know?"

He chuckled. "Well, it doesn't take someone who is *fey* to foresee what she would say. That is what most people consider good fortune. She tells people what they want to hear." The sound of a cantering horse could be heard approaching the gig from behind and Rose watched as Sterling neatly tooled the little carriage to the far side of the road to allow the faster rider to pass on the narrow tract.

"But it wasn't just that she said I would marry soon, but . . . that I would wed someone titled and wealthy like . . ." Rose's voice petered out. She did not even want to mention the earl's name.

"Like Cherrington." His tone was almost a snarl when he said the name, but after a moment he continued in his normal voice. "Remember, there are hundreds of other titled gentlemen of England, my lady. These Gypsies are cunning in plying their trade. She would see all members of the gentry as desiring to marry wealth and titles. It would be a safe prediction. That is certainly in the minds of most females."

"But she did not know I was female."

In the darkness he glanced at her briefly before returning his gaze to the road. "Perhaps not, but an advantageous marriage is rather universal for males and females."

"Well, I do not wish such a marriage." Rose enfolded her arms to ward off the chill that seemed to race through her despite the temperate climate of the summer night.

"And why is that, Lady Rose?" To her surprise she found he'd taken his gaze from the road and stared at her.

"Money and a title do not ensure happiness in marriage. My mother did her duty and it did not prove to make her happy, Sterling. In the end her money was squandered and she had little to treasure, save her children. She was quite determined that I should not suffer the same fate, but I fear she did not survive to stay my father's greed. Between Robert, my father, and Cherrington I have come to realize there is little about gentlemen and their dealing with females which I respect. I merely wish I might never hear the word marriage again."

Rose suspected she'd shocked her companion for he fell silent. Marriage was the only respectable goal for gently bred females. Yet most had some say in that choice or why else did parents allow them a Season? She was to be sold to the highest bidder. The thought made her stomach roil.

"You are merely tired . . . my lady. You cannot judge all men by the few who have touched your life. Nor would you wish to spend the remainder of your days perpetuating this hoax to avoid wedlock. Bound to your bed during the days and your nights . . . spent like a wraith stealing about your own home. There has to be some solution to your current problem and I suspect it will come from a place you least expect. I would urge you to be patient and I am certain you will yet find happiness with the help of those who care about you."

Before Rose could respond, the approaching rider came out of the darkness and barreled past them.

He peered at them with undue interest, barely able to keep his seat on the horse. Remembering her situation, Rose turned her face toward Sterling. Instinctively he put one arm round her and drew her close as the traveler rode by them, disappearing from sight.

For a moment she nestled into the security of his embrace. How could it be that Sterling was everything her father was not? He made her feel safe. He made her feel as if she had worth without profit for himself. But she had to admit that he made her feel far more than that. There were no daughterly feelings for the man who held her. Even now her heart seemed to beat faster at his touch. After the rider passed, she reluctantly straightened, and the man beside her went back to managing the reins.

Sitting there listening to the clip-clop of the horse's hooves taking her back to her prison of a bedchamber, Rose knew an urge to weep. Where would help come from to rescue her from this situation? Her only friends were in no better situation than she. "What other choice do I have but to continue to deceive my father? Happiness is not likely to be a consideration . . ." She couldn't finish when her throat constricted due to tears.

Beside her Garth's hands tightened on the reins, and he cursed his dilemma. The urge to reveal himself was strong, but his duty to his family could not be ignored. At present she was in no imminent danger of being forced to marry. Besides, he was uncertain how she would handle the fact that he would be accusing her brother of thievery. She had quite enough to worry about without adding that to her burden. If the need arose, he would tell her the truth, but for the present, he would continue to search for his family's treasure. "Do not lose hope, Lady Rose. Things are never as bleak as they seem. Remember you are not alone. Benson and I shall keep you safe."

The lady wiped her tears with the sleeve of her coat. "Oh, do not mind me. I fear I am being missish. 'Tis as you say, I am overtired. I won't endanger your position with my father nor Benny's. If the worst happens and I am revealed, I shall do what I must."

Garth wondered what that meant—marry or run away. But before he could question her the sound of a second rider approaching from the front echoed in the night air. Within minutes he could see the traveler, whose horse ran past at breakneck speed, hunched over his animal. Hairs on the back of Garth's neck stood up. Was that not the man who'd passed them earlier going in the opposite direction?

"Did that rider look familiar?"

Lady Rose shrugged. "I fear I scarcely paid attention. Most people look alike in the moonlight."

Garth snapped the reins of the gig, urging the horse to go faster. Something about two riders in so close a space of time did not suit him. It was near midnight and not noon. There should be few people out riding these remote roads.

The rapid speed of the gig in the darkness made it impossible to miss the worst of the ruts and the jarring became pronounced, yet Rose sat beside him holding on without the least complaint. Wary, Garth angled his head to listen behind, ever alert to danger. He detected the faint sound of hoofbeats coming after them. All the night needed was for them to be robbed by a highwayman. He urged the horse to go faster. Minutes later the gates to Denham

Hall came into to view. He tooled the little gig straight between the moss-covered griffons on the stone pillars, along the drive and up to the front door, not caring that one of the servants might have returned early and could see them. He wanted Lady Rose safely back inside.

He reined the horse to a halt. "I shall return this rig to the Brown Pigeon."

"Thank you for taking me to the fair, Sterling." She climbed down and moved toward the front door.

"Lady Rose."

She looked back at him. "Don't worry about the fortune-teller. Whatever she said, it was all a lot of nonsense."

"I can only hope." With that she turned and entered the front door.

Perhaps it was fatigue that had dampened her spirits so but more likely it was that cursed fortune-teller. He should have stopped her from going into the tent. Whatever the woman had said it had convinced Lady Rose that the battle was lost. He would have to speak with Benson in the morning. They must come up with a plan to put Lady Rose out of the marquess' reach permanently.

The whinny of a horse near the front gate brought Garth from his musing. Was the stranger who'd past them still lurking nearby? Garth patted his coat for the small pistol which he'd secreted before they had left for the fair. Lady Rose might not realize the danger of traveling about at night, but he knew that highwaymen and footpads still plied their trade with frequency. The gun was there and easy to reach. He urged the horse back up the drive, alert to any movement as he passed through the gates. But there was nothing but the whisper of the wind off the moors.

The trip back to the Brown Pigeon was uneventful and he returned the hired gig without incident. As he strode along the road to Denham he suspected Lady Rose's dark mood had made him see danger where none lurked.

Vitas crouched behind a pile of crumbled stones as the small gig came bowling out the front gates of the estate. He could make out little detail about the driver, all he knew for certain was the female was no longer in the vehicle. He'd had his doubts when he'd climbed on the horse they used to pull the caravan and hied after the two. Fearful that he'd lost them he'd pressed too hard and overtaken them on the road—a dangerous miscalculation—but the darkness had hidden his identity. Still the mistake had proven a good thing, for he'd seen with his own eyes the loose blond curls of the chit as he'd ridden past. So his mother had been correct. What he had to do now was find out the name of the estate and the name of the chit.

He moved to where he'd hidden Obelisk. His father had given the horse the odd name because the animal preferred standing around like a monument to cantering. The mad ride from York had nearly killed the old hack. She stood with her head hung down and her sides heaving.

A dilemma faced Vitas as he mounted. Should he go back to York with little information about the mysterious female or to the inn he'd passed a few miles back? Shifting uncomfortably on the swayback mare, he decided even a hedge tavern would be preferable than to ride all the way back to town on a horse with no saddle.

"Walk on, Obie." He kicked the horse's sides and the spent animal mustered a slow gait.

Within thirty minutes he'd safely slipped into the stable at the Brown Pigeon unseen, Obie left hobbled to graze on the moors. He found a spot of clean hay to spend the night without laying out any blunt. In the morning he'd visit the public room of the inn and strike up a conversation. Vitas has done it before when times had been hard and housebreaking had been the only option for ready blunt to silence his haranguing mother. There was nothing like a friendly innkeeper to learn about a neighborhood. By the time he returned to his mother he would know everything there was to know about the lady in boy's clothing.

Eight

Rose closed the door to the front hall, then sagged back against the oak wood. Sterling was correct. She couldn't waste her life hidden in her room, hoping her father would abandon his plans to marry her off for money. She'd been a fool to think this masquerade of hers was anything but a delaying tactic to buy her time. If nothing else, tonight had shown her there was a whole world out there to experience, both good and bad. Her father's need for money would not go away, and she was his deliverance from his straitened circumstances. That was not going to change no matter how long she stayed in her room.

She could no longer afford to sit idle and hope things would get better. Unless she was willing to marry as her father dictated, her only recourse was to leave Denham Hall. The mere thought made her shiver with fear.

Her gaze was drawn again to the lovely portrait of her mother and she moved in front of the image, wishing things were different and her mother were with her to guide and protect her. Staring at her mother's face, the defiant glint in her eyes and the stubborn set of her chin which the artist had captured, Rose suddenly remembered her mother's favorite Shakespeare quotation, something she always whispered before disregarding one of the marquess' unreasonable demands. "Courage mounteth with occasion."

Would her courage mount in her time of need? Would she be able to leave the safety of Denham Hall behind without a feather to fly with?

Her gaze roved over the picture, then locked on the lovely pearl necklace her mother wore with pride. The rope of pearls had been a gift from Lady Denham's father on her wedding day. Her mother had fought bitterly with the marquess over those pearls, when he'd wanted to sell them to cover a particularly bad run of luck. She had insisted that something else must be sold for they were intended for Rose. Her father had finally acquiesced and sold one of his hunters instead. The pearls were Rose's to do with as she would. Might they be the solution to her lack of funds? She could live comfortably hidden from her father for years on the proceeds from such a fine necklace. Perhaps she could even invite Sarah or Ella to live with her in a secluded cottage somewhere she would never be found. Then a worrisome thought occurred. Were the pearls still hidden in her mother's desk where they'd been when she departed for school? She would have to find them and . . .

"You are back safe," Benson's voice sounded from the top of the stairs, causing Rose to start.

Her old nurse held a candle and a look of relief relaxed the lines on her face. Yet even in the soft candlelight, Benson looked every one of her sixty-odd years. In that instant Rose knew that she must not endanger Benny's position here at the Hall. The woman had a comfortable sanctuary in which to live out her life. She was far too old to be dragged from pillar to post in the dead of night. Or to live by her wits until Rose sold the necklace then sought a safe place to hide. She decided she would have to go alone. As intimidating as the possibility of departing without her nurse was, the future no longer seemed so grim. The necklace and what it would mean for her future made her smile. Her mother would help her even in her absence.

"Sterling did as he promised and I am home safe."

When she mentioned the butler, Rose knew she must be careful. Sterling would stop her if he discovered her plan. There could be little doubt that both servants had done more than enough to protect her from her father, but she would not draw them any further into her scheme. Once she departed Denham Hall and her father's initial displeasure was spent in one of his normal rages, their positions would be safe.

Nurse eyed her closely as she came down the stairs. "You appear to have enjoyed your trip to town. What did you see?"

Rose had to be careful. She mustn't let her elation at her new plans overwhelm her. Benny might try and stop her should she realize Rose's intentions.

"Oh, it was quite amusing. I saw all kinds of wonderful things." She reached into her pocket. "And, as promised, I brought you a treat." Pulling out the sweetmeats, she unfolded the handkerchief and presented them to Benny.

The old woman eyed the candy with bemusement. She hadn't seen the girl so elated since before she went away to school. Perhaps the visit to the fair had been just what the girl needed.

"Shall we go to bed?" Rose asked, then she began to chatter about everything she'd seen as she led the way back up toward the room. The one thing she didn't mention was the fortune-teller. The very thought of the woman's prediction still made Rose fearful, despite Sterling's assurances.

The hour was late, but Rose wanted to find the necklace at once. All she would need to do was to wait until Benny fell asleep then she could go in search of the pearls. About to open the door to her room, Nurse put her hand on Rose's arm.

"You have not forgotten your bargain, have you, my lady?"

"Bargain?

"To remain indoors for the next month and out of trouble. You gave your word to me and Sterling."

A heaviness rushed back into Rose's chest. She had forgotten that she'd given her word as part of the bargain to go to the fair. Could she endure another month of utter solitude? Her immediate thought was to ignore her pledge, but how could she when Benson had done so very much to help her? It would be the worst betrayal. The very thought of another month made her want to shout, but she would keep her promise. She reminded herself that in thirty day's time she would be free and would have honored her promise to Benson and Sterling.

Sterling! His name sent a shiver down her spine. She could no longer deny a distinct attraction for the handsome butler. Was it because he was the only man in her life who showed the least sign of caring about her welfare, or was it those amazing blue eyes that looked at her with such intensity? She pushed thoughts of the man aside. She would be leaving in thirty days and then it would no longer matter.

"I will not break the bargain, Benny."

"I knew I could trust you, my lady. But you do have

a few days respite until the servants and his lordship return. You needn't stay quite so close to your bed during this time."

Rose fully intended to take advantage of Benson's offer. The women entered the bedchamber and Nurse prepared for bed but Rose picked up a book and sat beside the nearby light, pretending to read.

"Do you not intend to retire ?" Benson asked warily.

"I fear I have been up late so many nights that I am not sleepy." In truth, she was too excited about how the necklace would change her financial situation to sleep yet.

The old woman watched Lady Rose through narrowed eyes a moment. Having just received Rose's assurances that she would not leave the manor the old nurse seemed to come to some decision. She climbed under the covers and within thirty minutes, her snores could be heard from the trundle.

Noiselessly tugging her door closed, Rose slipped down the hallway to her mother's apartments. She stepped into the large room and her brace of candles lit the lovely gold and green bed hangings and matching wall covering. Strangely, the scent of her mother's perfume lingered. A flood of wonderful memories washed over Rose, followed by an ache of grief. This was no time for her sentimental longings. She moved across the room to the rosewood secretaire and set the candles aside. She opened the drawer. To her utter relief the carved wooden box was where it had always been kept.

She lifted the lid and her hands began to tremble as a flash of despair raced through her. The velvet-lined box was empty!

* * *

Garth locked the front door to the Hall. He was exhausted. It had taken him thirty minutes to return the gig and walk back to Denham. Had Lady Rose and Benson retired? Had Rose finally accepted that the Gypsy was no true fortune-teller? Or would she toss and turn, worrying about her fate? Perhaps he should broach the matter again on the morrow and try to convince her the woman, like most of her ilk, was a fraud.

The Hall remained shrouded in silence, only the ticking of the longcase clock could be heard. Despite his fatigue, Garth had no intention of letting a perfect opportunity to search for the chalice pass.

He casually tossed his hat on the table then picked up the candelabra beside the door. Making his way upstairs, he strode quietly down the long hallway not wanting to wake the two ladies who were sleeping nearby. He had progressed only a quarter of the way toward the young lord's room when a noise caught his attention. The sound of weeping could be heard from one of the nearby rooms. Puzzled, Garth stepped toward the sound, but it was a room he knew to be empty since it was the former mistress' apartments. He put his ear to the wood and listened. The heart-wrenching sound came from within.

He opened the door and discovered Lady Rose, her head bowed and her shoulders shaking with grief. She stood beside a lovely rosewood desk, a small box clutched in her hands. Thinking her reliving the grief of the loss of her mother, he moved closer to offer her comfort. She heard his footfalls and looked up. Tears on her cheeks glistened in the candlelight. In all that she had sustained at the hands of her father, he had not seen her so utterly devastated. Without thinking of the consequences he sat his candelabra on a table and moved to her.

The pain etched on her lovely face tore at his insides. But before he could say a word, she choked out, "He sold the one thing my mother left me. He sold her beautiful pearl necklace."

Without hesitation or thoughts of his assumed role, Garth drew her into his arms, wanting only to comfort her. "Are you certain someone else did not move the necklace? Perhaps to a safer place?"

She melted into his embrace, burying her face in his jacket. She shook her head. "No one save my father would have touched the pearls. All the servants knew it was my mother's wish that I have them."

Garth had little doubt that the marquess had sold the pearls. Outrage burned deep within his chest. What could he say to ease her pain?

"Rose, I . . ." he started, but there was nothing he could say to justify what her father had done. Perhaps because of the slip of the tongue to use her name, she leaned back and their eyes locked. Something ignited between them so intense the air seemed to quake. Garth's mouth closed over hers, gently at first but soon a growing heat took hold. The lady's arms slid up and round his neck as she responded to his heated kisses with a fire of her own. A need grew stronger within Garth to possess her.

An ormolu mantel clock chimed the hour of midnight which brought him to his senses. He released her and stepped back, angry that he'd taken advantage of her in such a manner. Lady Rose's cheeks were flushed and she appeared breathless. Her green eyes were dazed with emotion as she stared back at him.

What had he been about kissing her in that manner? She was an innocent and he was not here to involve himself in some clandestine intrigue. She seemed to possess some strange power that drew him to her as no other woman ever had.

The sounds of a door opening echoed in the hallway, then moments later Benson appeared in the late mistress' doorway. "There you are, my lady. I was so worried when I awoke and found you gone."

In a husky voice, Garth said, "Take her to her room, Benson." Without another word he turned and exited the room. Making his way down to the butler's room, he chided himself again for his conduct upstairs. He had set himself the task of protecting Lady Rose on the night he had given her a promise not to tell her secret. He suddenly wondered who would protect her from him?

"Is something wrong, child?" Benson stepped to where Lady Rose stood staring after Sterling disappeared through the doorway.

Wrong did not even begin to express how she'd comported herself only moments before. She had not only kissed one of her father's servants, she had enjoyed the event, nay even behaved like the most wanton female. Although dismayed by her behavior, she realized that Sterling had come to mean far more to her than a mere servant. He had become her companion, protector, and friend.

Yet every tenet taught her told her that servants were a separate class and one did not cross that barrier. It was never something truly spoken about even with her friends at school, merely an understood fact of life for the members of Quality. Her father and brother believed and lived the tenet, but did she? She had seen little in them to make her think that as gentlemen they possessed superior qualities to Sterling or any of the Hall's staff. In fact, she'd seen little to make her think there was much estimable in either of her relations.

After the death of her mother, Chalmers, Benson, and the other servants became like her family. They cared about her and she them. How could she think of such people as an inferior breed simply due to an accident of birth? Without a doubt, their new butler was superior to her family both in conduct and honor.

Her thoughts were full of Sterling. He'd almost kissed her before their ride that night, but he'd only been trying to make a point. This kiss was far different. A shiver of delight raced down her spine at the memory of his mouth over hers, the pressure of his chest against hers, and the strong beat of his heart in unison with hers.

Aware that her old nurse eyed her curiously during her long silence, Rose gathered her wits. Remembering the reason she'd come to her mother's room she said, "Forgive my distraction, Benny, but my father has struck me another stunning blow. I have discovered he sold Mother's pearl necklace." She extended the empty box.

Benson's brow puckered. "But she meant you to have—what am I saying? Of course what her ladyship desired would mean little to him where money is concerned. Well, my dear," the old woman slid an arm around Rose's shoulders, drawing her from her mother's room, "there is little you can do about the necklace tonight. Come to bed. You look positively burnt to the socket."

Rose allowed Nurse to usher her back to her room. While the old woman engaged in a diatribe against his lordship, Rose silently donned her night rail then climbed into bed. The loss of the necklace seemed to pale in the aftermath of Sterling's kiss.

In the darkness, her fingers came up to brush her swollen lips. She couldn't deny that she wanted him to kiss her again and again. But then was that not what love was all about?

Rose sat up with a start. She was in love with Sterling.

"What's wrong, child?" Benson sat up on her trundle and peered at the young girl in the dark.

Rose wasn't ready to tell her old nurse what she herself still could not fully fathom. "N-nothing, I thought I heard . . ." she remembered what Sterling had told her about Robert's room, "a rat but it must have been my imagination."

"Rats! No such thing, of that I'm certain. You are just overtired."

"You must be right. Good night, Benny."

Rose lay back on the pillow, but sleep would not come. Her night was spent pondering one question. What had the kiss meant to Sterling? A mere dalliance, a consoling embrace, or a heartfelt gesture of love?

By noon the following day, Vitas was back in York. The swaggering young Gypsy, full of information as well as a great deal of ale from the Brown Pigeon, found his mother in their caravan dozing on her bed. As soon as he opened the door she sat up, her turban askew and her dyed locks a dull, brittle color in the morning light. He informed her of what he had learned.

"The Marquess of Denham, you say." Madame Suldana licked her lips with greedy anticipation. Visions of purses full of coins whirled round in her head. "And this girl is his daughter you think?"

Vitas stuffed a piece of hard cheese in his mouth and took a swig of wine. "Didn't say that."

Madame slipped from the large cot at the rear of the caravan and loomed over her son in the small space. She had been waiting for him all night. How dare he come sauntering in here at noon? Later she would make him pay for worrying her. For now, however, she wanted to know all that he had learned. "Who is she then?"

He eyed his mother, ever wary of her Romany temper. "Don't know. Lord Denham *has* a daughter, 'tis true, but that one's injured. Thrown from a horse almost a fortnight ago. Ain't never woke up according to the innkeeper. Just lays in her bed with the servants hovering round her. General agreement among the lads at the Brown Pigeon is that the girl will cock her toes up afore summer's end. Rumor has it the marquess was about to marry her off to some old platter-faced earl for a fortune. They say her father fell into a passion when the sawbones said she might never wake." Vitas was tired and hungry. He suspected his mother had prepared nothing for them to eat. "I reckon the female dressed as a man what paid ye a visit must have been a maid from the Hall. Ain't no other female in residence but servants and the hurt girl."

"That was no maid, *fiú.*" Madame Suldana slumped into a nearby chair and pondered all her son had said. Those were not the hands of a maid. There was not a single callous or abrasion. But who was the chit? She kept turning the circumstances about in her mind, trying to understand why a gently bred female would have arrived in disguise from a house where there was only one female of that ilk and she was in her bed, senseless—unless . . . A wild notion settled into Madame's thoughts. A young girl about to be forced to marry an old dotard. Any young woman would detest the very thought of such a union. How far would this girl go to stop her marriage? Could it all be a trick? Certainly the one who came to her tent in male garb didn't lack for boldness.

The very idea seemed fantastical, but Madame's devious turn of mind had no problem accepting such deceit, especially for females. Life was difficult and sometimes a lie was all that could protect a woman from a man's whims. Had she not pleaded illness on many a night when her late husband had come home amorous, stinking of stale ale and sweat? Had the girl pulled the wool over everyone's eyes to avoid her fusty old suitor?

A smile split the fortune-teller's face. This was even better than she'd imagined. If it proved true, Madame rubbed her hands together with glee, she might never have to read another palm for the rest of her life.

She began to straighten her turban. "We must go back and find our little gentleman. Unless I miss my guess, Denham's ailing daughter is not so sick as everyone's been led to believe. You must break in and pay the young lady a visit. Find out if she was our young lad."

Vitas choked on the last bit of cheese. He had no objection to breaking into fancy houses. He'd been doing it since he was twelve, but going into the upstairs bedrooms of ladies of Quality might get him caught. He didn't relish the idea of getting his neck stretched. "But, *Anyu*, I don't see any profit . . ."

"Of course, you don't. I am left to think of everything. Get Obie hitched to the caravan. We shall find a place to camp near Denham Hall."

"But I only just returned and . . ." His mother smacked him on the head, letting him know how serious she was. With a tired sigh, he climbed out of the caravan to do as he was bid.

Denham Hall lay still and quiet much of the following morning, rain pelting the windows in heavy torrents. With the absence of his lordship and most of the servants, along with the late night had by all the remaining residence, there was no need to be up and about early.

After a restless night, Garth arose by ten, determined to put all his energies into the search for the chalice. He didn't want to think about his conduct toward Lady Rose the previous night and the best way was to keep busy. To his chagrin, he found Benson in the kitchen brewing a pot of tea, worry lines etched deeply round her mouth.

Despite his best intentions of putting Rose from his mind, he worried about how his conduct had affected her. "How is Lady Rose this morning?"

"I don't think that child slept a wink." Nurse poured the hot water into the pot which held the tea leaves, then set about slicing a loaf of bread. She handed the first piece to the butler. "I—I don't know what new thing has begun to worry her, but I fear that she is once again contemplating the thought of running away."

Garth took the proffered slice, but froze at the woman's words. "Did she say something?" Had he frightened her with his ardor? Gently bred females were not used to such handling and especially by one they thought a servant. He might have to tell Lady Rose who and what he was. He wouldn't risk her dashing off alone due to his foolish lapse of judgment. If she were determined to leave, he could take her to his family in London. Not that his parents would understand or approve of such a decision, especially when he arrived without the chalice and with the sister of the man who'd taken the cup.

Benson interrupted his musings. "It wasn't what she said, merely the way she's stopped speaking altogether after she found her mother's necklace gone, then her restlessness. I could tell something was clearly on her mind and it disturbed her greatly. Perhaps the futility of this charade is weighing heavily upon her and she can think of no other alternative. Leaving has been in her mind all along and now . . . I think she has lost all hope."

The idea of Rose alone and helpless in some city like York or London sent a cold chill down his spine. Poverty and death were a daily part of life in such towns. "We mustn't let her do anything so foolish. Shall I speak to her?"

A strange need to see her awakened in him. Not only to reassure her that he wouldn't press his advances on her again but to make her promise not to leave the safety of the family estate. But then she wouldn't see Denham Hall as safe as long as her father plotted her marriage.

The old woman shook her head. "Perhaps later. She dozed off before I came down. I'm hoping a bit of sleep will revive her spirits. I have begun to think this is all my fault."

"How so, Benson?"

"I made her pledge not to leave that room. I kept

going on and on about the bargain she'd made with us when she returned from the fair last night." Nurse poured out a cup of tea, handing it to him. "I, who knows what a lively creature she is, asked her to do something that she would find nearly impossible. That on top of her father's injustice is what made her toss and turn all night. I just know she will do something desperate."

Guilt sat heavily in Garth's chest. The old woman was taking the blame for something he might have done. Still he couldn't bring himself to tell Benson about kissing Rose. Instead he offered a solution. "Perhaps we should make an exception." He arched a brow at Nurse.

"What do you mean?"

"Allow her outdoors when it's safe." Seeing the look on Benson's face, he hurriedly added, "Nothing quite so dangerous as racing across the moors, but perhaps a walk in the garden after dark. There is a lovely little gazebo near the small lake which cannot be seen from the house nor the stables. What harm could there be to take her down there after everyone is abed?"

Nurse puckered her lips in disapproval. "I cannot like her taking such a risk, but I suppose I shall have to allow her some leeway or . . ." She didn't have to finish the sentence. They both knew what might happen. Lady Rose, in desperation, might leave, permanently.

A knock sounded on the rear kitchen door, startling the pair. Torn between his blasted duties and his need to help Lady Rose, Garth said, "Keep a close watch on her. We wouldn't want her to do anything rash. Tell me when she is awake. I shall come up to see her as soon as I am free."

That proved harder than Garth would have expected. Per his lordship's direction, several deliveries arrived that day despite the rain. Primary among them was the wine merchant's wagon with two scrawny lads who managed to break several bottles on the stairway to the cellar, which worried them not the least. After unloading the large foragon, they shrugged their shoulders and suggested a maid was better suited to cleaning up the broken glass and the muddy footprints.

Unwilling to ask Benson to come down and do the task, Garth found himself in his shirtsleeves mopping the cellar floors. He'd scarcely put the mops away when a man who announced himself as "Blocker's Baize" arrived, with a lad holding a bolt of fabric. Looking around the great hall in an assessing manner, he informed the butler he'd been given instructions to replace the worn green baize on the billiard table. Garth escorted him to the Games Room.

No sooner had Mr. Blocker taken out his tape measure than a foppish little man smelling of tobacco arrived. He produced four alabaster jars of his lordship's favorite snuff. He demanded to see where his produce was to be stored, for he had his reputation to think about and he would not tolerate Lord Denham proclaiming he'd given him a tainted blend.

Garth was tempted to box the pompous little man's ears, but in his forced role, he ushered the tobacconist into the wood-paneled smoking room. The man tested the windows and inspected the fireplace, then he gave Garth a great many instructions about how to keep the mixtures dry in such cursed weather. When the man stopped and fingered his lordship's brandy decanter as if he intended to sample the liquid, Garth made short work of his visit and marched the fellow to the door and bid him good day.

Standing in the great hall, Garth shook his head in dismay. He was appalled at the shocking way in which Lord Denham had squandered his winnings. Wine, a reworked games table, and powdered tobacco were hardly pressing matters when the estate was so wanting in all other aspects and many of the local merchants had not been paid in months. They had been reduced to using only meat from the Home Farm since the butcher refused any further deliveries until the estate reckoning was settled.

A crash of breaking glass, then a great deal of shouting made him sigh with frustration. In the Games Room he found Blocker screaming at the young boy who had knocked a small figurine from a table. No sooner had the butler arrived than the merchant proclaimed it to be a worthless bit of glass. Garth made no comment as he stooped to pick up the pieces. The porcelain figure was not of great value but certainly more than the lad could afford to replace on his meager salary. Convinced that he would only be making trouble for the young lad, Garth moved to put the pieces of the statue in a burred walnut commode with inlaid doors, but when he tugged on the decorative handles, the cabinet would not open and there was no key in the lock. He tried one of the drawers below the double doors, and it slid open. He put the broken figure inside then closed the drawer but eyed the locked double doors thoughtfully.

What could be in the cabinet, and where was the key? Wingate had spent a great deal of time here in the Games Room since he'd been home. Had he secured the chalice there and removed the small brass key to keep it safe? The only way Garth would be able to know was to open that cabinet but it would have to be later, after Blocker and his young assistant were gone and the ladies upstairs were retired for the night.

It was well after five when Garth ushered the man and his lad from the manor. He stood in the hallway and pondered what he should do first. He wanted to speak with Lady Rose and make certain he hadn't frightened her last night. But his sense of duty told him to break into the cabinet in the Games Room first. What he needed was a tool to pry open the doors. He hurried down to the kitchens and to his dismay found Cook, wet from her hike from the Brown Pigeon. She stood removing her rain-soaked bonnet.

"Good day to you, Mr. Sterling."

"Mrs. Whitby, I didn't expect anyone back until Thursday." Disappointment gnawed at Garth. He would have to delay his search of the cabinet until late that night.

"Nor had I planned to return until then, but to be honest, my sister's children are enough to try the patience of a Saint and as anyone who knows me is aware, I'm no such thing. Thought it was best I spent the remainder of my holiday here where I might enjoy a smidgen of peace and quiet."

Garth cursed the unknown nieces and nephews of Cook. He couldn't risk prying open the cabinet but he could finish his search of Wingate's room on the same old pretext. He politely welcomed the woman back insisting she not worry about duties in the kitchen while she was still on holiday, then excused himself with his pressing duties.

He made his way to the great hall and was about to mount the front staircase when an insistent knocking began at the front door. The time on the mantelpiece clock showed it to be almost six. Surely no merchant would arrive this late, for most country homes kept early hours. On opening the door he discovered a rider with an express mail from Lord Cherrington. After paying the man, Garth closed the door and looked at the letter.

What had the earl to say? Was he returning or had he found another female that suited him? Garth turned the letter over and over in his fingers. He couldn't imagine the man finding anyone superior in looks and breeding to Lady Rose, but he suspected that any young pretty female would do for the old man.

There was only a moment's hesitation before Garth strode to the library. After a brief search, he found a knife in the top drawer of Lord Denham's desk and gently lifted the seal without breaking the red wax. The contents of the letter was too important to Lady Rose's future to leave unread. He unfolded the note.

Cherrington's nearly illegible scrawl announced he would arrive at Denham Hall on Friday. He had purchased a Special Licence and, if Lady Rose was once again herself, they could be married in the nearest chapel on Saturday. He had pressing matters in Northumberland and could not delay while the banns were read.

Garth crushed the letter in his fist. Memories of Rose, soft and passionate in his arms the night before flooded his thoughts. She deserved better than an old man for her husband, better than a loveless marriage and he would see that she got her chance.

Lord Denham would return on Friday as well. Garth reckoned he had one full day to find the chalice. After that he intended to take Lady Rose into his confidence. If she wanted to leave Denham Hall, then he would take her and they would depart before anyone returned.

Once the decision was made, he tossed the crumpled missive in the fireplace and headed upstairs, straight to Lord Wingate's room.

Nine

The curtains were closed against the darkness by the time Lady Rose finally awoke that evening. The restlessness of the previous night had left her exhausted and to her dismay she'd slept away the entire day. No doubt her body had grown accustomed to the change in night and day. On sitting up in bed, she found herself alone. But she was not unhappy at her solitude. She needed to sort out what she should do about her feelings for Sterling.

The question haunted her as she climbed out of bed and dressed in one of the gowns Benny had reworked, a pale blue muslin dotted with white flock. Rose wasn't sure why she bothered to change, but in the back of her mind lingered hope that Sterling would come to her and explain last night's embrace. She might wish for more than a mere explanation, but she didn't dwell on such foolish hopes.

After brushing her hair and tying it back from her face with a blue ribbon, she went to the window and looked out. The continuing rain obscured the distant moors. Only an occasional flash of lightning brightened the gardens at random intervals. Perhaps the rain-veiled landscape was just as well. A prolonged look at the lovely hills would serve only to remind her what she could not have, her freedom.

Rose pondered the idea of going to the kitchens, but her pledge to remain in her room weighed heavily upon her, so instead she picked up a book to read while awaiting Benson's return. Yet Rose could not concentrate on *The Lady of the Lake*. She settled into a chair, the slender book open in her lap. Her thoughts returned to Sterling. Why had he kissed her? Had he only meant to comfort her after she'd become so distraught over her father's theft of her mother's necklace? She closed her eyes and relived every glorious moment of the embrace.

An innocent she might be, but instinctively Rose knew there had been more to his kiss than solace. Had he too experienced the same building of tension and excitement? Her whole being had tingled with a piercing need for him to hold her closer, to kiss her again and again. Her cheeks warmed at such thoughts.

Benson interrupted Rose's reverie when she arrived with a tray of tea, tiny sandwiches, and macaroons. "Oh, you are awake, child. Forgive me being away so long, but Cook has returned and since you were sleeping I sat and shared a cup of tea and some gossip about her sister. How are you feeling?"

Rose shrugged and lifted the book. Since she hadn't confided to the woman about Sterling, she didn't wish to share the gamut of emotions she was experiencing. Not wanting to ignore the woman, Rose stuck with a safe topic. "I am still very angry with my father about the necklace, but you needn't fear I shall do anything rash. I gave you a promise. You will have your thirty days of proper behavior." She attempted once again to read the opening lines.

"Well, my lady, Sterling and I have discussed your . . ."

Rose dropped the book to her lap. "You discussed me with Sterling?"

"Of course. He is as concerned about you as I am. We feel that, as long as you are careful, you can move about the Hall at night. Once things settle back to normal and Lord Wingate and his friend return to London, you might even walk to the gazebo near the lake on some nights. That is, on the nights Sterling is willing to stay up and escort you."

Rose casually turned the page without giving the words on the page a single glance. The thought of walking with Sterling in the moonlight beside the lake made her heart race. "I should enjoy such an outing." She paused a moment, then asked, "What think you of our new butler, Benny?"

The old woman busily poured a cup of tea and set sandwiches on a plate distractedly. "Well, there is no denying he's far too young to be a proper butler. Why, I think Chalmers himself was over forty before he earned such a lofty position." Benson paused a moment and stared into a darkened corner of the room as if looking into the future. "And decidedly too handsome."

A smile came unbidden to Rose at the old woman's observation. "You think him handsome?"

"I may be old, child, but not blind. But a comely face is no good thing in a butler I can tell you. Much too distracting for the younger female staff members. Cook says that Meg and Nell have positively wasted hours in front of the nearest looking glass, not to mention running to Sterling for every little question. Perhaps more work might get done if he married one of those witless girls." Benson went back to her task, her thoughts on the subject spent.

Sterling married to a pretty house maid! That gave

Rose a decidedly low feeling. She accepted the plate and bit into a sandwich with little enthusiasm, but she couldn't have told anyone whether it was cucumber or watercress, so preoccupied was she.

Benson began to move about the room straightening things as she chattered about the details of Cook's trip. Once she exhausted that subject, the old woman began to recount all the merchants who'd visited the Hall that day, going into detail about the repair of the old baize on the billiard table and the wine merchant's lads having an accident in the cellars. It seemed his lordship truly had a run of luck at the Gold Cup.

Rose only half listened. She couldn't put aside the idea that one of the house maids might ensnare Sterling with her wiles. He wouldn't be the first man who succumbed to a determined female, never mind that Meg and Nell were neither sirens of great beauty nor intellect.

A sudden memory flashed though her mind of Sterling's reaction after he'd kissed her. He had become stiff and reserved, leaving her without a word. There could be little doubt that a strong sense of honor forbade him to dally with his master's daughter. She sighed. Was there some unwritten butler's code about such things? Even if he cared for her, it might take years for him to overcome those boundaries and declare his true feeling. She didn't have that kind of time. Unless she wanted to remain locked in her room until he realized his true feeling would not be denied, she would have to do something unconventional.

Never one to shy away from a difficult task, Rose came to a decision. She wanted to know just where she stood with the man she loved. If that meant she must break all the rules of Polite Society, then so be it. She would run Sterling to grass and tell him her feelings.

Rose scrutinized Nurse thoughtfully, then came up with a plan to slip away from the woman's watchful eye. She put her unfinished meal on the table. "Benny, would you object if I slipped down to the library and found something else to read? This poetry is quite the most boring I've read."

Nurse looked up from the bed where she was straightening the linens. A frown puckered her lined brow, but she seemed to see something on Rose's face that made the tiny line disappear. "I suppose there is no danger. Cook retired to her room before I left the kitchens and Sterling won't bother you."

With a casualness she was far from feeling, Rose asked, "Where *is* Sterling?"

"I cannot say for certain, but likely he has retired to his rooms as well. There will be much for him to supervise since the remaining servants return on the morrow."

That was all Rose needed to hear to cement her decision. She must speak with Sterling tonight, to let him know that, if he loved her, she would forsake all for him. A sardonic laugh bubble up inside her as she slipped into the hall. There was only a miserable marriage to Cherrington in her future, or if she ran away, a life of servitude. She might need that argument to convince him that she would be sacrificing little if he wanted to marry her.

It was strange that she should be thinking of marriage after just having told Sterling she didn't wish to wed. True, she didn't want the kind of marriage her mother suffered nor the kind of marriage her father intended for her. But the thought of spending the rest of her life with Sterling gave her hope that she could be happy.

A lone candle illuminated her way. She paused at the head of the stairs to listen, but only the howling of the storm outside filled the great hall. She shouldn't be going to Sterling's room, but what else could she do? Another laugh escaped her. About to propose marriage to the family butler, her priority was already out the window.

A tremor of nervous excitement raced through Rose as she hurried down the stairs. When she reached the black and white marble floor a draft from under the front doors snuffed out her candle. The sudden darkness didn't frighten her, but she paused so her eyes could adjust to the inky blackness.

A flash of lightning lit the great hall. Rose froze in horror. Through the archway of the Grand Salon she saw the silhouette of a man trying to force open one of the drawing room windows. Someone was breaking into the hall.

She dropped her candle and fled down the hallway. All she could think was to get to Sterling. He would know what to do.

The darkness impeded her progress. She slowed and moved with her hands extended, fearful of bumping into something. She headed in the direction in which she knew the green baize door lay which led to the kitchens. As she moved along the passageway a glint of light showed from beneath the Games Room door. Someone must be in there. She halted in her tracks, looking back over her shoulder. To her relief the next flash of lightning showed the hallway remained empty.

Rose's attention once again returned to the beam of light glowing under the door. Who would be in the Games Room at this time of night? Benny had said nothing about anyone but Cook returning. There were only the four of them in the house and Benny and Cook were in their rooms which left only Sterling. But why would he be there at this time of night? Hadn't Benson said something about the billiards table? Rose couldn't remember, all she knew was that she needed to find Sterling at once. She softly pushed the brass lever and the door swung silently open. Relief and joy flooded Rose when she spied Sterling on the opposite side of the room—he stood hunched over at one of the room's cabinets. He appeared to be tinkering with the lock. Only one explanation came to mind—he was pilfering the contents. Suddenly the memory of his meeting with the young man at the fair flashed through her mind. The strange and secretive conversation she'd witnessed. What was Sterling involved in? Was the man at the window his friend? A sinking feeling settled into her stomach. Could she have been wrong about him?

"Sterling," Rose whispered his name with emphasis to get his attention, but not alert the housebreaker.

In front of the cabinet, the knife Garth had wedged between the locked doors slipped at the unexpected sound of his name. He turned to see Rose looking pale and nervous as she glanced behind her then back to the cabinet where he stood. Her eyes widened and distrust grew on her face. He suspected she realized he was breaking into the cabinet. He slid the knife in his pocket and quickly moved across the room to where she stood with a bewildered expression on her face.

"What are you doing in here?" There was accusation in her whispered tone.

"Not what you think." Seeing the doubt in her eyes he determined that now was the time to tell her. "I am looking for a jeweled, silver cup called the Chalice of Naples that your brother stole from Lord Buckleigh's house in London. It's the true reason I am here in Yorkshire." Seeing bewilderment on her face he was about to expand on the tale, then he frowned, " Why are you whispering?"

"My brother! A thief? Are you certain?" Then the slow screech of a long unused hinge sounded in the front hallway and she grabbed Garth's coat. "I came down to discuss last night," her cheeks grew pink, "but never mind that. There is a man outside of the Grand Salon trying to open a window. It sounds as if he's succeeded."

Garth didn't wait for further details. His hands closed over hers. "Go upstairs at once." He gave her a gentle push in the right direction, then retrieved his brace of candles and crossed the hall to the library. He opened the bottom drawer of his lordship's desk and pulled out one of the matched set of dueling pistols he'd seen his lordship displaying to one of his guest. To his consternation, Lady Rose appeared at his side.

"Go back to your room, Rose. I will come . . ."

"No!" She shook her head and bent to pull out the second pistol of the matched set. "You might need help if there is more than one housebreaker, and Padgett taught me how to fire one of these."

Garth almost protested, but thought it best to know where the fearless lady was at such a time. "Very well, but stay behind me."

She gave a nod of her head. "Oh, all right," she said as if making a great concession.

Garth smiled when she stuck close to him as they

moved along the hallway. He stepped into the Grand Salon and halted abruptly causing Rose to bump into him almost toppling the candles he held. The candlelight captured the figure of a very wet intruder who stood beside the window, putting a silver tray into a canvas sack. The man spun round as the room brightened. Fear was etched on his swarthy face.

"Stand where you are!" Garth barked aiming the pistol at the intruder even as he sat the candelabra on a nearby table.

The housebreaker dropped the bag and put up his hands. "I—I won't move, gov'nor."

Rose peeked from behind Garth and gasped when she saw the face of the villain. "You are the man at the fortune-teller's tent in York."

An evil grin lit the young Gypsy's face. "And ye are the young lad what visited Madame. Only ye ain't no lad. My *anyu* had the right of it. Ye be Lady Rosamund Dennison, and I reckon yer father and the old earl would be right interested to hear what devilish queer business ye and this here cully been about, especially since all the world thinks ye's ailing in bed." A stunned silence followed his announcement, then he added, "But for the right amount of silver I'll keep quiet about what I know."

Rose stepped back in fear, but Garth cocked the dueling pistol. "The right amount of lead will do the trick just as well, and your silence would be guaranteed to be permanent."

The Gypsy's gaze moved to the barrel of the gun and the smirk left his face. But before he could say a word the jangle of a team's harness could be heard approaching the Hall. Garth and Lady Rose exchanged a worried look. Without any urging, she hurried to the window and peered out. When a flash of lightning illuminated the visitors, she drew back from the glass. "I think it's Robert and Sir Marcus returned from the prizefight."

There was no time to ponder what to do, Garth barked, "Get to your room at once. I shall handle this matter."

She hesitated a moment, then the sound of the front knocker echoed in the great hall. With a final worried glance at the intruder, she laid the pistol on a nearby table then dashed out of the Grand Salon and up the stairs.

Before the sounds of her footfalls faded, Garth moved into action. He crossed the room to the Gypsy and kicked the canvas bag aside. He pressed the dueling pistol into the man's throat. "This is your lucky night, Romany, but you will have breathed your last if I ever see your face in Yorkshire again. You are not to come near Lady Rose or Denham Hall, nor speak one word to the marquess. Neither you nor the fortune-teller are to repeat anything you know to another living soul, or I shall see you hanged for thievery and blackmail. Do you understand?"

The man's head moved only slightly due to the gun under his chin, but the motion was clearly one of agreement. When a second banging of the door knocker began, Garth dragged the intruder back to the window through which he'd entered, then stepped back and motioned with the gun. "Be gone! I don't want to see you or Madame in York the next time I go there, or I shall visit a magistrate and see you both imprisoned."

Vitas needed no further encouragement. He scrambled back out the window and disappeared into the misting rain. Even if he had to gag and tie up his mother, they were leaving Yorkshire this very night.

Garth pulled the window closed and re-secured the lock. After a final glance out the window, he put the dueling pistol on the table and went to unlock the front door.

The two gentlemen pushed past him into the great hall, their driving coats dripping puddles on the marble floor. Lord Wingate removed his soaked beaver hat. "Where have you been, Sterling? A man's likely to catch his death of cold while you dawdle so long in answering the door."

"My apologies, sir. We weren't expecting you back so soon. "

Sir Marcus, drawing off his gloves, laughed. "Nor were we, but an embarrassing lack of funds changed our plans."

"The Ajax lost?" Garth's brows rose. He had followed in the newspapers the former slave Molineaux's attempt to become the English champion. While the man had been unable to defeat Cribbs, the reigning champ, the American had made short work of other opponents.

The baronet shook his head. "He won in just over an hour. Our wagers were profitable, unfortunately we left all of our winnings and more on the Faro table at Mrs. Duncan's."

"Never mind about that. I've a way to turn things around, Marcus." Lord Wingate appeared distracted as he tossed his cape to the butler. "Sterling, rouse Cook and see if she can provide us with something to eat, and light a fire for us in the library or we are like to catch a chill in these damp clothes." Without the least thought to the inconvenience he caused others, the gentleman strode off toward the library.

Sir Marcus handed his wet gloves, coat, and hat to Garth. "Anything will do Sterling. Don't have Cook go to a great deal of trouble, for it's late."

While the two young gentlemen headed for the library, Garth took one last glance into the Grand Salon. He hoped he'd made the right decision in letting the Gypsy go, but what other choice did he have? His gaze roved up the stairs and he knew he needed to speak with Rose to finish explaining everything to her. Things had been happening so fast, she'd had no time to absorb the information about her brother's thievery. Surely once she had some time to think she would want a fuller explanation. But that would have to wait, for now he must see to Lord Wingate and his friend.

Pausing outside her bedroom door, Rose clutched at her heart which hammered in fear and anguish. Her thoughts swirled in a maelstrom—the Gypsy might betray her to Lord Denham which would mean a forced marriage. And she hadn't even begun to grasp the meaning of Sterling's accusation against her brother. According to Sterling, Robert was a thief.

Sterling! The man had become so important to her. But who was he? Clearly not a butler. He said he had come in search of this missing chalice. Good heavens, was he a Bow Street Runner? She'd heard about the men from another girl at school who told the tale about her father having to call on Bow Street to retrieve a stolen diamond necklace. While Rose had never met a Runner, she had no difficulty in believing they were all tall handsome men of virtue who caught villains. But such a man would be no more acceptable to her family than a butler.

Voices in the front hallway echoed up the stairs. Rose smoothed her hair before entering her room. She mustn't appear nonplussed or Benson would be full of questions. Questions which Rose wasn't ready to answer. But she needn't have feared for the old woman lay slumped asleep in her chair, her needlework in her lap.

Rose paced the room nervously for nearly an hour wondering what had happened downstairs. Had Sterling been able to get rid of the intruder? Occasionally she would go to the door and press her ear against the wood, but there was nothing to hear. Frustration settled deep within her but she couldn't risk leaving her room. Would Sterling risk a visit tonight to tell her what had transpired after she fled? As the time passed, she finally decided that he might not be able to slip away from her brother and his friend. Perhaps she should prepare for bed. After all, Robert might stop at her room to ask if she'd improved and it wouldn't do to be caught unaware. Within minutes she'd donned her night rail and removed the ribbon from her hair, but still she couldn't sleep as worries about the Gypsy's threats filled her head.

When she heard her brother's voice in the hallway as he made his way to his bed, she dashed across her room and climbed into the large four-poster. She pulled the covers up to her neck and closed her eyes, but Robert moved on past her room without stopping to see how she faired. How foolish she'd been to think he might have the least concern for her.

The hands on the clock drew closer to two, yet still Sterling did not come. Rose realized it would be a very long night.

* * *

The return of Lord Wingate was decidedly inconvenient, especially with the other servants still gone. Garth found himself at the young lord's beck and call for most of the remainder of the night. After building the fire, he went to the kitchens and roused Cook, then helped the old woman put together a cold collation for the men. He urged the woman to return to her slumber and she happily padded back to her room. After delivering the meal to the library, Garth was ordered to the cellars for a new bottle of brandy, then to the Games Room for a deck of cards. He eyed the cabinet he'd been unable to open and promised himself to have another go at it later.

While the gentlemen played Piquet, Garth lit the candles in the great hall, fearful that one of the men might tumble down the stairs when they finally retired. He'd just finished the wall brace nearest the front door when a soft tapping sound made him stop and look around. To his surprise his brother's face appeared at the closest window.

Garth glanced toward the library, then strode to the front door. He opened the portal and stepped to the stoop. The rain had slacked to a fine mist. He noted his brother was again dressed in his usual fashionable garb. "Why have you come, Jack? Has something happened?"

"A letter from Father." Jack pulled the folded missive from his jacket. "Mother is ill. He wants us to return to Hillcrest as soon as possible."

Garth didn't open the letter, instead, he said, "She was in perfect health when we departed. Did he say if the illness is serious ?"

"A severe irritation of the nerves which her physician says only seeing us shall put to an end." Jack shrugged. "She must be bad for him to have sent for us. Or maybe he is losing patience, it has been taking so long." There was a hint of accusation in his voice, as if to question what his brother had been doing all this time.

Garth ignored the barb. "And what of the chalice? Are we to leave without finding it?" His mother had always been a bit high-strung but generally his father had been able to keep her on an even keel. A deep sense of failure flooded Garth. He'd been certain he could find the silver cup but he hadn't reckoned with the limitations his role as butler would put on him.

He didn't want to leave, but he couldn't refuse his father's entreaty to return home. There was Lady Rose to worry about though. Her situation was even more dire than when she'd first arrived home. The Gypsies knew her secret and might yet expose her despite Garth's threats.

"After Mother sees we are still in one piece, Father intends to put the matter in Bow Street's hands and hope for the best. I am putting up at the Golden Fleece and shall depart in the morning. Do you wish to ride back in my phaeton?"

Garth's mind raced. The thought of leaving Rose here at the mercy of her family was unthinkable. Her father would be merciless if he learned the truth about her pretense. His fists tightened when he remembered the abuse he'd witnessed, but that was quickly replaced by the memory of her in his arms, eager and welcoming of his kisses.

In a sudden bolt of understanding Garth realized his desire to stay wasn't just to protect her from physical danger. He loved her and wouldn't leave her behind.

"I have some things to finish here first. I shall

come as soon as I may, but assure Mother that I am well."

Jack was silent for a moment. "Does this have to do with Denham's daughter? I'm not blind, Garth, despite her disguise it was evident she is a beauty."

Before Garth could reply the door the library opened and he was forced to draw the door partly closed but not before he whispered. "Go, I shall see you in Berkeley Square within a few days." He shut the front door, then grabbed the candle snuffer which stood nearby.

To Garth's relief, the men paid scant attention to him as he stood stock still. They chattered about visiting York the following afternoon while they made their way upstairs, parting at the landing to go to their separate rooms.

Garth's father was demanding he return to London and without the chalice. Defeat had never been part of his thinking, so he had one last night in which to find the chalice. With no time to lose, Garth marched straight to the Games Room, closed and locked the door. He set to work on breaking open the cabinet. In a matter of minutes he'd pried the lock, and the doors swung open. To his disappointment, there was no chalice inside. Instead the cabinet was full of a collection of broken games, cracked billiard balls and generally the debris of years of a well-used Games Room. No doubt the servants used the cabinet to keep his lordship from knowing about the breakage.

Garth closed the cabinet doors with frustration and pondered what he must do. Over the course of the past weeks he'd searched every possible place and still had not recovered the chalice. As much as he hated to admit it, the possibility that they were wrong about Lord Wingate rose. Had he wasted his time here in Yorkshire while the real culprit had sold the cup. Perhaps his father was right, they should turn matters over to Bow Street.

Garth had to depart tomorrow, especially if his mother wasn't well, but not without Rose. Was she still awake? Likely she was frightened after the Gypsy's threats. She would wonder about his accusations regarding her brother and the stolen chalice. She would want answers and sooner than later. If he had come to realize one thing it was that she would slip out of her room in search of him if he didn't go to her. That would be too dangerous now that Lord Wingate was back.

He turned over the options in his mind. He loved Rose and if she would have him, he wanted to marry her. But it wasn't that simple. Lord Denham would do all in his power to stop him and force her to marry Cherrington. There was only one solution. They must marry at once. He knew his family would be shocked, but he had no other choice.

With his mind made up, Garth made his way upstairs, halting outside her door. He scratched softly on the wood, but there was no response. He couldn't knock for fear he would rouse Wingate, so he opened the door and peered inside.

A brace of candles burned on the bedside table, illuminating Rose, dozing in her bed. He stepped into the room and spied Benson, who also slumbered in a chair near the fireplace. Garth tiptoed to Rose's bed. For a moment he considered not disturbing her rest, but her beauty and innocence moved him to lean down and kiss her.

She woke and slid her arms round his neck, returning his ardor. Elation joined passion for Garth knew in that moment that she loved him. When he drew back happiness reflected in her eyes and she whispered. "You came."

"Of course, I came, my love." He edged back, not sure he could control his desire as he realized the sheer texture of her white muslin and lace night rail and her innocent willingness.

She reached to trace a finger across his lips then slyly announced, "I—I love you."

He trapped her hand and kissed her slender fingers. "I love you, too, Rose. I think I fell in love with you the moment I opened the front door and there you were in all your tousled splendor just returned from school."

"Oh, I don't think it was then for all I could see was disapproval in your eyes when you insisted I might want to tidy myself before I met my father." Mention of the marquess' name took the teasing light from her eyes. She sat up, her expression sobering. She glanced at her nurse, then in a whispered undertone asked, "What happened to that dreadful man in the salon?"

"He's gone. There is no need to worry about him." His finger traced the delicate line of her chin. "Rose, I must leave Denham in the morning."

She clutched at his hand. "D-did you find the chalice?"

"No, but this evening I received word that my mother has taken ill. I must return to London."

"Take me with you, my dear Sterling." Fear of being abandoned made her mouth tremble.

Garth brushed a curl from her cheek. "I won't leave without you, my love. That is why I came to you to ask you to marry me."

She threw her arms round his neck and pressed

close to whisper in his ear. "My dearest heart, I will proudly be your wife."

The softness of Rose against him sent a wave of desire racing through Garth. A desire that he couldn't act on yet. Needing to put a bit of distance between them, he clasped her arms and moved her back to look in her eyes. "Things are going to be rather difficult with your father."

She nodded. "I understand, but once we are married he might rail all he likes and it cannot hurt us."

"But I fear what I am going to suggest will cause a public scandal. It won't just be your father but much of the Polite World who will censure our conduct."

"What do you mean?"

"We cannot delay this wedding, my dear. We must be married before your father can learn where you are gone. Otherwise I cannot stop him from demanding your return should he track us down. What say you to Gretna Green?"

Rose's eyes widened then a smile tipped her lovely lips. "Married over the anvil? I cannot think of anything more exciting. Do we leave tonight?"

"I must arrange for a coach and team for our journey. I am without cattle and vehicle in my present post and I won't use your father's. I'll not give him an excuse to accuse me of thievery to have me put in the gaol."

She nodded, a thoughtful expression on her face. "May I bring Benny? Father might take his anger out on her when he discovers that I am not only in full health but have eloped."

"I insist you bring your nurse." He looked over at the old woman who stirred restlessly in the chair. "Are you sure she will accept this elopement?"

"I can make her understand." Rose smiled at him, her eyes shining.

Garth still had one matter to broach. "My love, there is the matter of Lord Wingate's theft of the chalice."

She sat back and plucked at her blankets. "I cannot believe he is so lost to honor that he would steal but then he has not fared well under my father's treatment either. I suspect his gaming debts are large or why else would he linger here in Yorkshire so long?"

A thought occurred to Garth. "Would you know of any place at the Hall where he could hide something like that? He would need privacy to pry the stones from the chalice. I have searched his room and most of the surrounding chambers but there was nothing."

Rose shook her head. "There are no hidden passages or such at Denham." Then she sat up. "But when I was a child I used to hide things that I didn't want Father to find in the Gazebo's cabinets. I will show you." She reached to throw back the covers but Garth grabbed her hand.

"Not tonight, my love, 'tis far too late and the weather is dreadful. There will be time enough in the morning." He pulled the blankets to her shoulders, pressing her back into the bed. He leaned over her and gave her a searing kiss which seemed to sap her strength. "You need your rest for the journey tomorrow and I must hire the carriage. We shall search the Gazebo before we depart."

Pushing aside the restraining blankets, she threw her arms round his neck. "Sterling, I—I hope you know that I shall have nothing from my father to bring to you once we are wed even were he to approve our marriage, which he won't." Then a smile curved her lovely lips. "Unless, you have some hidden legacy, like Chalmers."

It suddenly occurred to Garth that Lady Rose had no idea who he was. To her he was Sterling, a penniless butler, not a future viscount. Even so she had willingly agreed to marry him. She had fallen in love with a man not his title or wealth. His heart swelled with contentment and love.

"I want nothing from your father, I want only you, my love." He kissed her again then stood. He would explain everything to her later. "In the morning pack what you need for the journey. I shall arrange for the carriage to meet us at ten near the west gate. We must be gone by noon for your father returns tomorrow evening." He didn't tell her that Cherrington was to return as well and with a Special Licence. Such fearful news would ruin her rest.

Rose reached up and cupped his face to draw him back to her. Her lips met his and the embrace lingered, neither wanting to part from the other.

"Sterling! Lady Rose!" Benson shrieked their names in choked outrage, her hands gripping the chair where she'd been asleep.

The pair parted guiltily. Garth could see the disappointment and distress on Nurse's lined face. "Mrs. Benson, I . . ."

But she would have none of his explanation. In an instant she was in front of him. "Leave here at once. You have taken advantage of this sweet innocent child's situation."

Rose tried to explain. "Benny, I love . . ."

The old woman threw up her hands. "I don't want to hear any of that nonsense. You are the daughter of a marquess and he is a butler. That is like trying to blend oil and water. You would never fit in his world nor he in yours. Can you imagine him sitting at your father's table after having served there? Or you dining in the servants' hall? Use your head, my lady."

"But, Benny . . ."

The old woman took a breath and began anew, listing more of the ills of such a union.

Garth knew better than to try and interrupt a female before she'd spent her fury. So he crossed his arms and watched, amused at Rose's determined efforts to interject.

At last, after some five minutes, Rose found her moment. "Will you please listen! Sterling is not a butler!"

Benson's eyes narrowed. "Is he not? Well, you could certainly have fooled me."

Rose, incensed, said, "Well, he did, he fooled us all."

"So, Sterling, you came to Denham to purchase a horse and got lost in the kitchens and liked it so much you decided to stay."

Before Garth could respond, Rose again dashed to his defense. "He came because he is a Bow Street Runner on an important mission to find a stolen chalice."

Garth was as stunned by Rose's pronouncement as Benson. He'd had no idea that when he'd explained his true reason for being at Denham her fertile imagination had come to such a conclusion. Having seen the occasional runner, Garth chuckled at her mistake.

Benson, however, was not impressed. "Bow Street! A common Runner! Oh, and that makes a world of difference, my lady. I'm thrilled at his superior station in life," the old woman said, perhaps even more horrified than when she thought him a butler. Unlike her young charge, she'd encountered a Runner in her youth. Her memory was of a wiry little man from the depths of London's rookeries wearing ill-fitting clothes, with a penchant for peering at one with decidedly shifty eyes and an ever present Occurrence Book handy. The mind reeled at the thought of such an alliance.

A fire lit in Lady Rose's eyes. "Benny, I won't listen to another word. . . ."

"Ladies!" Garth realized it was time to intervene before things elevated to a shouting match and they woke Lord Wingate. "I am neither a butler, nor a Bow Street Runner."

Both women stopped and turned to him. Rose's face a picture of surprise while Benson's countenance was full of distrust.

"Then why did you come looking for Lord Buckleigh's chalice?" Rose asked.

"Because, I am his eldest son."

It took a moment for the words to sink in with each of the ladies. For Lady Rose there was complete bewilderment at her sudden change in situation, but Benson positively beamed. "Why, I always told Lady Rose you were the most commendable of fellows."

Rose's eyes widened at that statement and she looked at her old nurse as if the old woman had just told her to tie her garters in public, for she'd never praised Sterling in the least.

Ten

By six o'clock the next morning Garth was on his way to the nearest posting house to hire a carriage to carry Lady Rose and her nurse to Scotland. Armed with his true identity, he'd had little trouble convincing Benson that an elopement was the only solution to their situation. Both women had promised to be packed and ready when he came for them.

The slow but reliable Delphi was produced when he came to the stable and he headed to the Golden Fleece for a traveling carriage since the Brown Pigeon had no vehicle larger than the little gig. The trip was scarcely two miles, but after the storm of the previous day, the roads were muddy and the old mare shied away from every new puddle.

By eight he reentered the gates of Denham, anxious to take Rose away, but to his consternation, a carriage was drawn up in front of the stables. As he drew closer, he recognized Lord Denham's squat physique as he stooped to inspect a fetlock of one of two chestnut yearlings which the grooms held. Garth swore under his breath at such ill-timed bad luck. Their departure would have to be delayed until this evening to be safe.

Formulating a tale in his head to explain his trip, Garth rode straight up to where Lord Denham displayed his newest purchases to his head groom. The marquess' face exhibited shock at the sight of his butler on horseback, then the look quickly evolved to one of displeasure.

Garth dismounted. "Good day, my lord. You have returned early."

"And a good thing it would seem, Sterling. While the cat's away the mice will play, eh?" The gentleman glared at him. "Where have you been? I thought I was clear on your remaining at your post while I was away."

"So you did, my lord. But I was forced to take a quick journey to Thirk to see to my ailing mother. As you can see, I am back in time to see to your home-coming."

Garth could see the puzzled look on the face of Padgett, the groom who'd prepared his mount. No one could have ridden to Thirk and back in so short a time, but the man kept his tongue between his teeth.

Denham harrumphed, whistled to his hounds, then turned and strode toward the Hall. He settled in his library and after a flurry of orders, set to work on his breeding records, never remembering to ask about his daughter's health. Garth made no mention of the fact that none of the servants had returned, save Cook. Instead, he set about seeing to the gen-tleman's comfort all the while hoping that Benson might come down so that he could send word to Rose that their departure would be delayed from ten this morning to ten that evening, that is, if he could slip away and meet the coachman to pay him and ask him to return.

By nine, his lordship was ensconced in his break-fast parlor, enjoying a hearty meal. Garth slipped away to Rose and Benson to inform them of the change of plans.

When he stepped into the room he could see at once that the women had somehow learned of Denham's return. Rose stood looking out a window, dressed in an elegant gray traveling gown with black frogging down the front. He suspected the garment had been one of the former marchioness' since it fit far better than the blue one in which she'd arrived. Her blonde hair was drawn up into a cluster of small curls at the top of her head, making her appear quite the reserved young lady, not the madcap he'd come to expect. But perhaps it was her mood that created such a somber appearance as she stood in deep thought. The sound of the closing door drew her from her reverie and her green eyes brightened at the sight of him, but her spirits remained low even as she crossed the room to melt into his arms. "Whatever are we to do, with Father at home?"

"I fear we must delay our departure until after dark." He turned to Benson. "Can you go to the west gate and give this to the coachman?" He handed her a small pouch. "When he arrives tell him to return at ten this evening and there shall be another one just like that."

Benson clutched the leather bag, but did not leave at once. "Do you not think it best to leave this morning? I don't think his lordship will bother to come to visit Lady Rose. He won't have the least idea that she is gone."

"True, but he would certainly take note of a missing butler." Garth smiled as the old woman nodded her head. After a glance at the pouch as if she suddenly remembered her duty, she slipped from the room.

"Sterling, what about . . . ?" A thought made her crinkle her brow. "What is your real name?"

He gave a fashionable bow. "I am the Honorable Garth Sterling Fenton, at your service, my lady."

"Garth," she said his name shyly, then shook her head. "I fear you shall still be Sterling to me, my love."

"If you like, but it will be far easier when you are around family and friends who know me as Garth." He kissed her.

She sighed with pleasure then returned to her earlier question. "What about the chalice? We need to look in the gazebo before dark."

Garth took her arms. "It's not safe, Rose. If I get time today, I shall go there and search, but I won't risk your safety for the chalice. My father will turn things over to Bow Street." His disappointment at his failure laced his words. "If it's never recovered, I still wouldn't change a thing about my time here at Denham Hall, my love."

"But you came all this way and . . ."

"Not another word. I must get back. Thomas and the maids haven't returned as yet so I am acting as the entire staff. Keep to your room and I shall come for you tonight." He kissed her and departed.

After the door closed, Rose wandered back to the window and stared out at the lake. It wasn't that far away and there were no servants about. Clearly this chalice held some significance for his family. Why else would they have gone to such length to send their son into such a difficult situation?

Rose couldn't stand the idea that Sterling—no, it was Garth—would have been so close to recovering the cup and had given up the chance for her. The gardens were empty, the servants still gone, her brother and Sir Marcus rarely rose before noon.

What better time to go and search the gazebo than at present?

Determined to do what she could to find this treasured goblet before they departed Denham Hall forever, she went to the door and listened. Hearing not a sound, she opened it and peered up and down the hallway. Not a soul was in sight so she hurried past Robert's room, down the back stairs past Cook and out the rear door.

Garth slipped unobtrusively into the dining parlor and moved to fill his lordship's coffee cup. The marquess lifted his hand.

"I've had enough." He rose and tossed his napkin on the table. "I have several important business letters to write, Sterling. I am not to be disturbed for the next hour." He walked to the door, then paused to look back. "By the by, has anything changed with my daughter?"

"She is as she was when you departed, my lord." That was no lie.

The gentleman sighed then strode out of the room.

Garth went to the sideboard and began to put the dishes on a tray. He disliked doing kitchen duty. He almost wished the other servants had returned—he froze on that thought as he caught a flash of blond hair and a gray gown moving through the gardens.

Great heavens, Rose was out of her room and headed for the lake! He left the dishes where they were and hurried back down to the kitchens, where Cook watched in surprise as he dashed out the back door. Having never gone to the small lake before he took several wrong turns. He couldn't call out to her for fear someone would hear, but at last he overtook her some fifty yards from the lake.

"What are you doing here?" He grabbed her arm and stopped her.

"We must at least look in the gazebo. It won't take more than a few minutes." The rapid walk through the gardens had raised the color in her cheeks and she looked much like she had that first day he'd seen her.

About to protest, Garth halted when a tapping sound echoed on the breeze. It came from the lake. "Someone is in the gazebo."

"Shall we see who?" Rose forged ahead before Garth could protest, not that he would at this point. She was already outside her room and the chalice was too important to walk away from without giving his all.

They hurried along the path that led to the lake. Soon the slate roof of the gazebo came into view. It was an oblong structure, open all around with benches and a few cabinets built into the framework of the open exterior walls. It clearly was designed for parties to be held beside the lovely little lake. At first Garth thought the building stood empty, then he caught movement down near the floor on the far side of the open room.

Someone was crouched over an object of interest. Garth recognized the tousled blond curls of Lord Wingate as he worked diligently to pry a stone from the Chalice of Naples. Rage consumed Garth to see his family treasure so mistreated. Without a thought to the consequences, he raced toward the Gazebo.

But in his haste, his running footfalls alerted the young man to his coming. In an instant, Robert shoved the cup back inside a cabinet and slammed the door. By the time Garth mounted the steps into the building, Robert Dennison had moved to stand beside a rail as if he'd come to watch the ducks.

With feigned disinterest, he eyed the man he knew as the family butler. "Sterling, what brings you . . ." Then he caught sight of his sister peering round the end of the shrubbery watching him, suspicion etched on her face. "Rose?" He took several steps toward her as if not believing his eyes, then his gaze flew back to Sterling. "What are you doing . . . why is my sister not . . ." But before he could finish he found himself in the butler's strong grip.

"I should wring your neck, Wingate. If you've done anything to damage that cup, I shall thrash you within an inch of your life."

Barely able to speak, Robert tugged to break free even as he croaked, "How dare you lay hands on me . . . you country oaf!"

Rose hurried up onto the porch and went straight to the cabinet where they'd seen Robert stow the cup. She lifted it out, turning the chalice round as the jewels sparkled in the morning sunlight. "Why, it's beautiful, Sterling." Then she turned to her brother. "How could you become a common thief, Robert?"

Lord Wingate struggled for a moment and at last shrugged from Sterling's grip. "For your information, I didn't steal it, Dixon did." Seeing the doubt in her eyes, he whined, "It was a mistake, but what could I do once we reached Denham and he told me he'd filched the cursed thing? Besides, I haven't a feather to fly and just one jewel. . . ." His eyes narrowed, "But then you have much to explain yourself, dear sister. Pretending to be incapacitated when obviously you are not. And what are you doing out in the gardens with this, this *former* butler?" Clearly he meant to see that Sterling was fired after his rough treatment at the man's hands.

" If Dixon is the thief, Wingate, then why were you out here taking the stones?" Garth took the chalice from Rose and slowly rotated it to inspect the stones. The time in the gazebo cabinet had taken a minor toll in the form of tarnish which could be easily remedied. Other than that, the cup was in excellent condition, save several small scratches near one of the larger rubies.

"I don't have to explain anything to you, Sterling," he sneered.

"How would you like to explain it to the local magistrate?"

Robert straightened his cravat. "It's my word against yours. And who do you think they will believe?"

Rose gasped. "They will believe me, for I shall explain what you were doing."

Robert looked from his sister to the butler and back. "Oh, very well, it was Dixon's game. He keeps the bill collectors from the door with little things he nips—a snuff box, jeweled lorgnette or even the occasional purse. Then I had a particularly bad week at the tables and even a few baubles weren't going to set things to rights. I wrote and asked Father for an advance on my allowance but he ignored me, as usual. There was no way to avoid the debt, so I began to avoid my usual friends. That's when I accepted an invitation to dine with Buckleigh's youngest son."

Rose looked at Garth, but his gaze was riveted on her brother's face.

Robert continued. "While we were in the dining

room, Dixon slipped in to look for something and spied that magnificent cup. I'm not certain what he was thinking, but he came away with the thing and hid it in the boot of my carriage. He didn't even tell me until after we returned from Somerset what he had done, knowing I shouldn't be well pleased with such an valuable item. Too many questions and such. I didn't want to keep it but I'm so far up the River Tick I cannot think straight."

Rose reached out to put her hand on Garth's as a gesture for him to be merciful to her brother. The movement and the intimacy of the look which passed between the pair caught Robert's attention. He saw far more than a butler and a lady. There was a smoldering intensity in that look which spoke of deep emotions.

His sister and the butler! Revulsion and shame coursed through him that she had lowered herself to such depths. They would be the laughing stock of the *Ton* if this got about.

His face distorted with rage and he rounded on Rose. "Why, you common little baggage. I see what you have been about, pretending to be ill and all the while cavorting with a servant." He struck his sister's cheek.

This time Garth didn't stay his reaction to the assault on the woman he loved. He punched Wingate in the nose and sent the man hurtling into the wooden railing which gave way under the onslaught. The man fell through the broken balustrade and landed on the ground below.

In an instant Robert came to his feet, hatred in his eyes to be so treated by a man whose station was so far beneath him. Even as the blood streamed from his nose he shouted, "I shall make you pay for that, you lowly cur." His gaze flashed to his sister, then back at the man who'd bested him. "My father shall know what to do with you and your little doxy." He turned on his heels and raced back toward the Hall.

Garth swore under his breath. They were about to be revealed and Rose would be the one to pay the consequences. He grabbed her hand. "Are you unhurt?"

She traced her fingers over the red mark on her cheek. "I shall survive but Robert is about to tell my father I'm awake and embellish it with some dreadful tale about our so-called dishonorable conduct."

Garth looked down at the chalice, all the while his mind raced. "We must leave at once. Hopefully we can get to the carriage I hired before Benson sends them away."

"But . . ." Rose had no time to argue. Garth tugged her down the stairs of the gazebo. They hurried across the gardens to the west gate. Some minutes later, they arrived, breathless to find Benson seated on an old stump still waiting for the carriage's arrival.

On seeing them approach she rose. "What happened?"

"Robert discovered I'm not really hurt any longer, Benny." Rose looked to Garth then merely said, "He went to tell Father I am in love with Sterling."

The old woman's face blanched white. "We are finished."

Garth stepped to Benson and put a steadying arm round on her shoulder. "We are not. When the carriage arrives, we shall depart immediately. It will be at least an hour or more before they realize we are gone and longer still before they can start after us."

The old nurse wrung her hands. "How can we

leave? We have no clothes, or money and what about his lordship's horses? They will overtake job-horses in a matter of hours."

"The border is only a few hours away, Benson. Why, Rose and I shall be safely married long before Lord Denham figures out what has happened."

The sounds of the approaching carriage was a godsend. The vehicle drew to a stop and Garth urged the ladies to board. But Benson continued to protest that neither she nor Lady Rose possessed even a bonnet for the journey.

After a promise to buy them proper hats at the first safe opportunity, the old woman climbed into the carriage. Garth's conversation with the coachman involved the exchange of the small pouch. He then climbed in the large traveling coach which set out at breakneck speed for the Scottish border.

The marquess' roar could be heard all the way at the stables after he heard his son's tale of the liaison between his new butler and his headstrong daughter. Then he realized that all was not lost with his deal with Cherrington. Had the ungrateful jade allowed the man to ruin her? If she had so forgotten herself, he would still make her marry the old earl, even if he had to threaten everything and everybody she cared about to keep her silent about her wanton conduct.

But first he would put an end to that lying, cheating butler. He grabbed one of the dueling pistols from his drawer, determined to get things in hand. "Where is Sterling?"

Robert removed the handkerchief from his nose. "They were at the gazebo when last I saw them." His gaze moved to the gun and a satisfied smirk tipped his mouth.

Denham hurried to the lake, his hounds frolicking along at his heels, but the summerhouse beside the lake stood empty. He quickly went to the stables thinking Rose might have gone and requested his best mounts to flee, but no one had seen the pair. He ordered the grooms to search the grounds, declaring to everyone that the new butler had abducted his daughter.

For over two hours the gardens and stables were scoured and no trace was found of either Lady Rose or Sterling. When the head groom came to the library to report his results, Robert rose from a chair. "They can't have gone far on foot."

Lord Denham paced in front of the windows. "And where would they go?" But no one had ever bothered to question Sterling about where he was from. Then he remembered the butler's mysterious trip. But where had he been that very morning? Thirk, but that made no sense for the town was miles north of York. At last, the marquess said, "Go bring the girl's nurse. Surely she will have some clue where they might have gone."

Robert dashed up the stairs and went first to Rose's room, then to the attic rooms where the old woman usually slept, but again the room was empty. Where the devil was everyone? He hurried down to the kitchens where only Cook stood in front of the stove making treacle pudding.

"Where is Benson, Cook?"

"Why, she hurried out of here nearly three hours ago for a walk, my lord. I'm beginnin' to worry about her. Is there alt I can do for ye?"

Robert didn't even bother to answer the woman.

He dashed back up to the library where his father was impatiently waiting.

"Benson has disappeared as well."

The marquess swore, then walked to the window. "Where can they all have gone?"

Robert put his mind to the thing. He recalled the moonstruck looks Rose and Sterling had exchanged in the gazebo. This was no mere dalliance, the fools imagined themselves in love. "My word, you don't think the blackguard has taken her to Gretna Green?"

A second roar of similar volume emanated from the marquess. It took several minutes for the gentleman to regain his composure. "If he has, his wedding day will be his last day on earth." Denham turned to his son. "Go to the stables; have Kerr harness my fastest team to my curricle. We leave for Scotland in ten minutes."

Robert had no wish to race to Scotland after his fool of a sister, but the thought occurred to him that if his father killed Sterling, he might yet get the chalice back. Then he wondered how his sister and that cur had known the cup was stolen?

"Don't stand there like a statute, Robert. This involves family honor. We must go at once or we are likely to have a lowly butler claiming acquaintance to our noble family, or worse, trying to convince that fool Cherrington that his first born is truly his." With that the marquess swept from the library fully expecting his son to follow without protest.

Eleven

By four that afternoon, the Honorable Garth Sterling Fenton and Lady Rosamund Dennison stood over the anvil at the center of the Scottish village of Gretna Green while the blacksmith performed the short ceremony. Both the bride and her nurse wore rather odd bonnets, full of large wax fruit and feathers purchased from two old ladies who'd stopped at the same posting inn to change horses. Prim little spinsters, they had been unable to resist the exorbitant fee offered by the handsome young man for the two hatboxes strapped to their carriage.

Rose had protested being married in such a hideous hat, but Benson insisted that no proper female would be married without her head covered, and so the ceremony took place without delay. Yet the blacksmith's voice kept creeping up a notch as he seemed to have some difficulty peering at the feathery cornucopia while saying the vows. Finally, with a twinkle in his eye, he pronounced them husband and wife.

It wasn't until the marriage party repaired to one of the local inns and Rose was sitting in a private parlor that she fully realized she was a married woman. A flutter of trepidation raced through her. In truth she knew almost nothing of her husband, save his kind nature. Where would they live? What would his family think of her?

Garth entered after ordering a meal for their party. He gently tugged the hat from her blond curls, giving her a kiss while Benson stood nervously peering out the window. All Rose's worries melted away in his embrace. She didn't care about all those mundane matters as long as she could be with the man she loved.

"Well, my dear wife, I fear that our journey is not at an end."

"But, we are married. Can we not stay here for the night?" Rose was too tired to think about climbing back into the coach, and she wanted to spend time alone with her new husband.

Garth drew her to a bench on the far side of the private parlor so that his words could only be heard by her. "My love, I won't have my first night with my wife interrupted by her raging father." The look in his eyes was speaking as they roved over his beloved's face. " I think it best we journey to Carlisle for the night." He traced a finger along her cheek and she shivered with longing. "I shall leave Lord Denham a note explaining who I am and my direction. If he wishes to take me to task, let it be in my own home where you will be safe from him."

At that moment two maids entered the parlor with trays of food. The pleasing aroma reminded Rose how hungry she was. "Why Carlisle?" she asked as she surveyed the spread of roast chicken, creamed potatoes, and salad.

"We wouldn't want to cross paths with your father on the way back to London. We can veer west to Carlisle, spend the night, then set out first thing in the morning."

Rose's eyes widened. "We are for London?"

"Did you think I meant to take you all the way to Hillcrest with only the clothes you wear?" Garth laughed.

Rose should have been delighted at such a treat as visiting Town, but instead she was flooded with new worries. "We shall meet your family?" After he nodded she asked, "What will they think of . . . of our elopement? Of me?"

Garth gripped her hands which were nervously fidgeting with the frogging on her dress. "They will understand once everything is explained and will love you as I do. Then we shall post a proper announcement in the papers that we were married from Denham. Your father won't contradict the report. He will want no scandal. Come let us eat, we must be on our way soon."

Rose found comfort in his reassurances. With the resiliency of youth she stood and called to her nurse. "Benny, come and eat. I fear we must depart again."

The old woman turned from the window where she'd been on watch. "And a good thing, my lady. Your father will be here too soon for my comfort and I think it best we are nowhere to be found."

On that Garth was in total agreement. He didn't wish to have to face off against his wife's father in a duel, which, knowing Denham's uncertain temperament, might be a possibility. He insisted Benson join them and the trio partook of the meal. Afterwards, Garth penned a missive which he gave to the innkeeper, Mr. McKinney, to deliver to the Marquess of Denham. Within forty minutes of their arrival, they were ensconced in the carriage as it passed through the Sark Toll Gate then crossed the stone bridge. They were once again in England, heading first south, then taking the turn southwest toward the town of Carlisle.

Scarcely thirty minutes after the bridal couple had departed, a dusty curricle with a spent team arrived at the crossroad in Gretna. The larger of the two men climbed down and strode purposely toward the inn while the younger took his time, stopping to stretch and gaze around at the famed town.

His lordship entered the inn shouting, "Innkeeper, a word, at once!"

Not unused to dealing with irate parents and guardians, Mr. Mckinney came out and bowed politely. "Lord Denham?"

"Aye," the marquess replied warily. The fact that his name was known did not bode well.

The innkeeper handed him the missive. "Mr. Fenton requested that I give you this message, my lord."

"Who the devil is Fenton?" Denham snatched the note and broke the seal. He quickly read the neat lines, his face changing from anger to disbelief.

Robert stepped up and peered over his father's shoulder. "What is it, sir?"

The marquess rounded on his son. "Some nonsense about Sterling being Lord Buckleigh's son and a stolen silver chalice. What do you know of this?"

Robert, Lord Wingate, grew pale. Realizing that, not only was he not to recover the chalice, but he was likely to be exposed as a thief, he began to weave back and forth. His eyes rolled backwards and he collapsed in a heap on the floor.

Lord Denham scowled at the crumpled heap of his son. "Damnation! He's hollow as a drum!"

* * *

Some two days later the well-traveled carriage from the Golden Fleece drew to the curb in Berkeley Square. Within minutes the newlyweds and Benson were ushered into an empty drawing room by Hickam who could ill-contain his delight at the sight of Garth carrying the wrapped bundled.

"How is my mother, Hickam?"

"Soon on the road to recovery once she sees you, sir." Then his gaze roved to the females in the odd hats and his brows rose.

"This is my wife, Lady Rose, and her servant, Benson." Garth stepped to his nervous bride and slid an arm round her waist as she shyly greeted the servant.

Despite her strange appearance, Hickam forgot himself enough to smile. "Welcome to Buckleigh House, my lady."

Before their arrival could be announced, Lord Buckleigh and Jack strode into the room, having heard voices in the hall. His lordship moved to embrace his son. "Thank God you are home at last. Hickam, inform her ladyship that Garth is back and well."

The butler departed as Garth presented his father with the bundle. "We found it, sir."

Lord Buckleigh took the chalice and unfurled the wrapping. He held the cup up to the morning light and gave a sigh of relief. "It's unharmed." He turned back to his son and smiled. "Jack said you hadn't found it the last time you spoke. You have done well, son."

"Better than you think, Father. May I present my wife, Lady Rose, and her nurse, Mrs. Benson? Rose, this is my father and brother, Viscount Buckleigh and Jack."

Despite his surprise, his lordship stepped gallantly

forward and kissed his new daughter-in-law's hand. "I am certain there is quite a story here, but first let me welcome you to the family, my dear." Then he turned to the servant, taking in the years in her cup. "You are most welcome, Mrs. Benson. Hickam will show you to a room for I am certain you are tired."

The old woman bobbed a curtsey and withdrew to the hall to await the return of the butler.

Jack shook his brother's hand, his brow arched questioningly. "What happened after I left?"

Garth smiled down at Rose. "A great many things, but we shall explain later. . . ."

Before he could finish, Lady Buckleigh, attired in a lovely pink lace wrapper, hurried into the room and threw herself into Garth's arms. She was decidedly paler and thinner with dark circles under her eyes but he was certain she would quickly recover with both her sons at home and out of harm's way. Once again introductions were made and Lady Buckleigh embraced her new daughter-in-law with pure joy, never questioning how such a marriage had taken place, only that her fondest wish had been achieved.

"Oh, my dear child, you must be exhausted after your journey. Pray allow me to escort you to your room. Hickam will see to your luggage and—why, whatever is wrong, child?"

Rose blushed and looked to Garth.

"Mother, I fear she has no luggage."

"No luggage!" To a woman of fashion such a statement was unthinkable. "How is that?"

"We eloped and were forced to leave in a great hurry without even the ladies' bonnets."

A strange expression appeared on Lady Buckleigh's face. Garth was uncertain how his mother would handle such a scandal, but to his amazement, she went to the door and summoned a footman. "You must go for Madame Colette at once and tell her it's the utmost emergency." After the servant hurried away, she returned to Rose and eyed the funny bonnet. "Men just don't understand how important is a lady's wardrobe." She untied the bonnet and removed it. "I hope you will be guided by me, child. We cannot have Madame seeing such an atrocity." She took the offending article as if it possessed unwanted creatures among the fruit and handed it to Hickam.

Rose grabbed the ugly bonnet. "It is rather hideous, but I should quite like to keep it, my lady, since my husband gave it to me."

"What were you thinking, Garth?" Her ladyship eyed the creation with horror.

"Benson convinced me that any bonnet was better than no bonnet."

Lady Buckleigh shuddered. "Well, I suppose." With one last glance at the hideous article, she insisted her new daughter come upstairs to rest before Madame Colette arrived. Garth urged her to go.

But before Rose departed she turned to Lord Buckleigh. "May I resolve some of my questions about this whole scheme, sir?"

He smiled at her. "Of course, my dear."

Rose looked down at the bonnet in her hands not seeing the fruit as she pondered what she wanted to know. She looked back at his lordship. "What do you intend to do about my brother?" Despite his rough treatment of her, she could not help but worry. In many ways her father's treatment of Robert had brought him to such ends.

Stepping forward, Garth said, "I should tell you, Father, that Rose figured out where the chalice was hidden. She led me to it, even knowing her brother might be implicated."

Lord Buckleigh lifted the family heirloom and was quiet a moment as he took in its splendor. "We have our treasure back, my dear. There will be nothing to do. I shall let the marquess handle his son's disgraceful conduct."

Rose sighed, knowing that her brother's punishment at their father's hands would be harsh, but at least he wouldn't be sent off to Newgate. There was little else she could do in her present situation. One other matter nagged at her, though. "Can you tell me where Chalmers is and how did you get him to leave his post at Denham Hall?"

He smiled. "My solicitor went to Yorkshire. He sent the man a message summoning him to a local inn where he produced a letter by a long lost relative who had left the man a cottage and an annuity for the remainder of his life if he could take up residence immediately. It took some persuading, but Chalmers left in Mr. Hooper's carriage within the hour. He is happily gardening on my estate in Wiltshire."

Garth nodded his approval. "He is at Hillcrest. You will see him again soon."

Lord Buckleigh smiled. "I do believe him quite content, my dear."

A sense of gratification settled into Rose. She might be forever estranged from her father and brother, but she would have Benny and Chalmers with her at her new home. On that happy thought she allowed Lady Buckleigh to escort her upstairs.

Garth poured wine into a glass, then moved to the rear window to await his wife. He'd spent the remainder of the afternoon recounting his tale of life at Denham Hall to his father and brother. Both agreed there was little else he could do but take Rose with him. Jack soon bid his father and brother good day and went off to join his friends. As Lord Buckleigh was about to depart and allow his son to change for dinner, he paused at the door.

"Do you love her, son?"

"With all my heart, sir."

The gentleman smiled and nodded his head before closing the door.

The scent of the roses in the garden wafted on the evening breeze, reminding Garth of her love of flowers and he couldn't wait to show her the gardens at Hillcrest. He hadn't seen her since that morning when his mother had spirited her upstairs, and he longed to hold her in his arms. After his father left, Garth sent her a private message to meet him in the Blue Parlor early if she could slip away from his mother before dinner. They had things to discuss. Did she want a honeymoon trip? Or did she prefer to stay and see the sights of London before he took her to Hillcrest?

The sound of the front knocker made Garth look to the mantelpiece at the clock. Who would be calling at seven? Then he heard Lord Denham's raised voice in the hall. Somehow he hadn't expected the man to come here after what had been revealed in the letter.

Garth set his glass aside and strode into the front hall to see a red-faced marquess bellowing at Hickam. The butler stood firm in refusing the man's orders.

"I demand to see my daughter, at once."

Garth drew his hands behind him, afraid the urge

to throttle the marquess might get the better of him. "Hickam, I shall speak with Lord Denham in the library."

"You blackguard," Denham shouted on seeing Garth. "I should . . ." The marquess took several menacing steps to where Garth stood, unfazed by his lordship's posturing.

At that moment the library door opened and Lord Buckleigh appeared. "Lord Denham, I never thought you would dare to show your face in my home after what your son did!"

The marquess' bluster faltered. "My son? What is some bauble compared to the fact that your son ran off with my daughter? Do you think I shall be deterred by some nonsense about Robert? I demand to see Rosamund."

Garth took a step forward. "You cannot demand anything of my wife, sir."

From the head of the stairs Lady Rose appeared, having heard her father's voice. The viscountess had not wasted the afternoon with the modiste. The young bride was beautiful in a pink silk gown with white sarcenet overskirt, her golden curls drawn away from her lovely face, a set of her ladyship's pearls round her neck.

All eyes were on her and a moment of silence fell in the hall.

"Why did you come, Father? I am no longer of any value to you now that I am married." Her gaze moved to her husband and the pair exchanged a smile as if there was no one else in the room.

Lord Denham's eyes narrowed. "There you are wrong. These people owe me for taking you from your family. There are settlements."

Rose's eyes flashed fire as she looked back at her

father. "You sent me to school and forgot me," she started down the stairs even as she continued, "you arranged a marriage without the least thought about my wishes, and you struck me when I protested." Her hand came up to her cheek as the painful memory returned. "You have been no true father to me and you think you deserve a settlement especially after what Robert did to the Fentons?"

"He did nothing, it was that fool Dixon."

Rose pressed her point as she came face to face with her father. "Yet he intended to sell the jewels for his own benefit, never thinking to return the chalice to its rightful owner. He has no more integrity than . . . than his father when it comes to money."

"How dare you speak to me . . ." Lord Denham drew his hand back to strike her, but Garth was there in an instant. He grabbed the marquess' arm, then shoved him backward into the wall.

"Never again raise your hand to my wife if you value your neck, Denham." Garth put his arm round Rose. "You are not welcome in this house, sir."

Hickam stepped forward and opened the door. The marquess looked at everyone. "I shall go to my solicitor and see . . ."

The viscount came to stand beside Rose and Garth, creating a united front. "And if you do I shall inform Society to lock their doors against Lord Wingate's thievery."

Lord Denham froze. Even the hint of such conduct by his son, true or not, would ruin Denham Stables. His dark eyes burned with outrage as they rested on his daughter. This was all her fault, but they had him. At least he didn't have to live down her marriage to a servant. Realizing there was nothing else he could do, his shoulders sagged.

"Bah! You are welcome to her. She is nothing but trouble." On that, the marquess hurried down the stairs and climbed in his carriage with a shouted, "Home."

Rose's cheeks flushed pink as she turned to her father-in-law. "I am sorry to have subjected you to such a scene."

His lordship leaned forward and kissed her cheek. "You needn't apologize. I am proud to claim such a brave and beautiful young lady as my new daughter." He smiled, then added, "Now I must go and see what is keeping your mother."

The gentleman hurried up the stairs, but they both knew he departed to give them some time to themselves. Garth led Rose to the Blue Parlor and closed the door while she moved to the windows to look out at the small garden.

He came up behind her. He slid his arms round her and she leaned her head back against his chest. They stood in silence as the tension flowed from them.

When at last Rose accepted that she would never have to see her father again she sighed. "I feel like I have been living in a nightmare since I came home from school."

Garth tilted her chin upward and kissed her. "Then wake up from your bad dream. It's over and you have a new life with me."

Rose smiled up at him. "Would you think me strange if I asked if we might go to Hillcrest as soon as I have replaced my wardrobe? Just you and me?"

Garth's arms tightened. "I would never think you strange, my love, and Hillcrest is exactly where I should like to take you. I need to take hold of the reins of the estate once again, for Father prefers to remain in Town."

Rose turned and entwined her arms round his neck. They had so much to learn about each other. She wanted to tell him about Sarah and Ella and her promise to invite them to stay, but for a few weeks she wanted him to herself. "You will always be my beloved Sterling."

"And always yours to command, my lady." His mouth closed over hers and they enjoyed their solitude until Lord and Lady Buckleigh joined them nearly thirty minutes later.

ABOUT THE AUTHOR

Lynn Collum lives with her family in Alabama. She is currently working on the third installment of her fairy tale regency trilogy, WHEN THE SLIPPER FITS (Ella's story), which will be published by Zebra Books in April, 2003.

Discover The Magic of Romance With

Jo Goodman

__More Than You Know $5.99US/$7.99CAN
0-8217-6569-8

__Crystal Passion $5.99US/$7.50CAN
0-8217-6308-3

__Always in My Dreams $5.50US/$7.00CAN
0-8217-5619-2

__The Captain's Lady $5.99US/$7.50CAN
0-8217-5948-5

__Seaswept Abandon $5.99US/$7.99CAN
0-8217-6709-7

__Only in My Arms $5.99US/$7.50CAN
0-8217-5346-0

Call toll free **1-888-345-BOOK** to order by phone or use this coupon
to order by mail, or order online at **www.kensingtonbooks.com.**
Name_____
Address_____
City_____ State _____ Zip _____
Please send me the books that I have checked above.
I am enclosing $_____
Plus postage and handling* $_____
Sales tax (in New York and Tennessee) $_____
Total amount enclosed $_____
*Add $2.50 for the first book and $.50 for each additional book. Send
check or money order (no cash or CODs) to:
Kensington Publishing Corp., 850 Third Avenue, New York, NY 10022
Prices and numbers subject to change without notice.
All orders subject to availability.
Check out our website at **www.kensingtonbooks.com.**

The Queen of
Romance

Cassie Edwards

__Desire's Blossom $5.99US/$7.99CAN
  0-8217-6405-5

__Exclusive Ecstasy $5.99US/$7.99CAN
  0-8217-6597-3

__Passion's Web $5.99US/$7.50CAN
  0-8217-5726-1

__Portrait of Desire $5.99US/$7.50CAN
  0-8217-5862-4

__Savage Obsession $5.99US/$7.50CAN
  0-8217-5554-4

__Silken Rapture $5.99US/$7.50CAN
  0-8217-5999-X

__Rapture's Rendezvous $5.99US/$7.50CAN
  0-8217-6115-3

Call toll free **1-888-345-BOOK** to order by phone or use this coupon to order by mail.
Name_____
Address_____
City_____ State _____ Zip _____
Please send me the books that I have checked above.
I am enclosing $ 109.22
Plus postage and handling* $_____
Sales tax (in New York and Tennessee) $_____
Total amount enclosed $_____
*Add $2.50 for the first book and $.50 for each additional book. Send check or money order (no cash or CODs) to:
Kensington Publishing Corp., 850 Third Avenue, New York, NY 10022
Prices and numbers subject to change without notice.
All orders subject to availability.
Check out our website at **www.kensingtonbooks.com**.

More Zebra Regency Romances

___A Taste for Love by Donna Bell $4.99US/$6.50CAN
     0-8217-6104-8

___An Unlikely Father by Lynn Collum $4.99US/$6.99CAN
     0-8217-6418-7

___An Unexpected Husband by Jo Ann Ferguson $4.99US/$6.99CAN
     0-8217-6481-0

___Wedding Ghost by Cindy Holbrook $4.99US/$6.50CAN
     0-8217-6217-6

___Lady Diana's Darlings by Kate Huntington $4.99US/$6.99CAN
     0-8217-6655-4

___A London Flirtation by Valerie King $4.99US/$6.99CAN
     0-8217-6535-3

___Lord Langdon's Tutor by Laura Paquet $4.99US/$6.99CAN
     0-8217-6675-9

___Lord Mumford's Minx by Debbie Raleigh $4.99US/$6.99CAN
     0-8217-6673-2

___Lady Serena's Surrender by Jeanne Savery $4.99US/$6.99CAN
     0-8217-6607-4

___A Dangerous Dalliance by Regina Scott $4.99US/$6.99CAN
     0-8217-6609-0

___Lady May's Folly by Donna Simpson $4.99US/$6.99CAN
     0-8217-6805-0

Call toll free **1-888-345-BOOK** to order by phone or use this coupon to order by mail.

Name_____

Address_____

City_____ State_____ Zip_____

Please send me the books I have checked above.

I am enclosing	$_____
Plus postage and handling*	$_____
Sales tax (in New York and Tennessee only)	$_____
Total amount enclosed	$_____

*Add $2.50 for the first book and $.50 for each additional book.

Send check or money order (no cash or CODs) to:

Kensington Publishing Corp., 850 Third Avenue, New York, NY 10022

Prices and numbers subject to change without notice.

All orders subject to availability.

Check out our website at **www.kensingtonbooks.com**.

BOOK YOUR PLACE ON OUR WEBSITE AND MAKE THE READING CONNECTION!

We've created a customized website just for our very special readers, where you can get the inside scoop on everything that's going on with Zebra, Pinnacle and Kensington books.

When you come online, you'll have the exciting opportunity to:

- View covers of upcoming books

- Read sample chapters

- Learn about our future publishing schedule (listed by publication month *and author*)

- Find out when your favorite authors will be visiting a city near you

- Search for and order backlist books from our online catalog

- Check out author bios and background information

- Send e-mail to your favorite authors

- Meet the Kensington staff online

- Join us in weekly chats with authors, readers and other guests

- Get writing guidelines

- AND MUCH MORE!

**Visit our website at
http://www.kensingtonbooks.com**